Beau-Laid

Justin Bourne Boring

Congratulations!!
I hope you Enjoy!!
—JBB

LDP
Literary Dreams
PUBLISHING
Making literary dreams come true

Literary Dreams Publishing

Published by Literary Dreams Publishing

Cover Design by Justin Bourne Boring

www.literarydreams.com

Contents

This book is dedicated to my beautiful wife and wonderful step-daughter who helped me through this entire publishing process. Thank you honey for supporting and encouraging me to write about love!

Chapter One

Logan Lepozod

Logan

My birth mother and biological father were worth less than ash. I never knew them. According to my exceptionally wealthy uncle, they had, without warning, selfishly, callously and carelessly abandoned me with him when I was still an infant. They presumed his money would make it easier for him to care for me.

My uncle was from my mother's side, so we did not share the same name. Also, they had been estranged for decades, so he did not consider me family. It was a fact he constantly reminded me of and never let me live down. He was a cruel and bizarre man.

Uncle Effram would drape me in the finest clothes, but only when I was in school or when he paraded me around in front of his people. The rest of the time I wore what he called a "uniform," which was the most basic of clothing. At a very young age, I wore this uniform when performing millions of various tasks around the house and estate. Sometimes the "tasks" were questionably dangerous. During the brutal winters up north, I scarcely had enough clothing to keep me from freezing to death when shoveling snow.

Uncle Effram also furnished a very elegant room for a young boy, and when there were visitors, I was allowed to stay there; otherwise, I had to sleep in a cold, barren storage area in the cellar. He would take me to the finest restaurants but restrict me to eating next to nothing.

He constantly pointed out to anyone that would listen that I was destitute and that he had taken me in because his heart was so big.

Needless to say, in his words, he had risen to the call of benevolence as any compassionate, moral person would. However, missing from these myriad testaments of kindness and philanthropy was the reality that I was a malnourished, sometimes well-dressed slave who was a prisoner within the finest home of an upper New York state mansion.

I quickly learned that speech was my enemy in the house of Effram; unless, of course, it was to praise him. Fortunately, my dedication to studies and oil painting earned me a millimeter of benefit in my uncle's mind. He respected that I knew my place, especially when it came to his circle of aristocracy.

Uncle Effram was particularly impressed with my oil paintings, which he often showed to affluent guests, who would proceed to "Ohhh" and "Ahhh" over them.

When I turned ten, I was sent to boarding school. I would never once return to the mansion from that point forward. Uncle Effram paid extra to have me live year-round at school, alone and isolated. I never once received any present, card, or letter from Uncle Effram- or anyone else for that matter. The only correspondence I ever received was six months before I was to graduate the 12th grade at boarding school, and it was from the Les Beaux Arts de Paris, a top-tier art university in France. The letter informed me that I had been approved to attend the school and that all tuition had been paid in full. I had a modest allowance that would be distributed to me monthly by the Dean, and extra monies had been paid in order for me to lodge there for the entire duration of my studies. Past university, I presumed I was on my own, and I would be right.

During my third year at the Les Beaux Arts de Paris, I received an official letter that informed me of dear old Uncle Effram's passing. Despite being worth many millions, he left me absolutely nothing. This did not upset or surprise me in the slightest. I had no illusions about the kind of person he was; regardless, I was eternally thankful for my education. I owed him that, I guess.

Upon graduating from university at the top of my class, I had many opportunities afforded to me thanks to my grades, talent with oil painting, and art curating. This was the first step in making many millions for myself.

I was invited to join the Whitney Museum Biennial, thanks to several of my oil paintings garnering some attention by serious collectors. After winning the very illustrious Bucksbaum Award earlier in the year of 1998, due to my involvement with the Whitney Museum Biennial, I was soaring!

A mere five months after winning the award, and only seven years after graduating, I sold my first painting for $500,000. I was disappointed I had fallen short of the million dollar mark, but it would only be a few months later when I crossed that milestone.

Eventually, I had my own gallery in the heart of Soho called Lepozod, my self-created last name. It featured all my paintings and sculptures, as well as many of the art world's finest contemporary talent. It was touted as the most esteemed contemporary art gallery on the east coast. Once I had real tangible wealth, stature and was established in the upper echelon of aristos, the world began to bow at my feet.

It tickled me to think of how Uncle Effram would undoubtedly be proud and take full responsibility for my success, had he been alive. Despite his cruelty, he was due some of that pride for bankrolling my education. His inhuman treatment also had been my first big lesson in the world, and it taught me strength, drive - and cruelty.

Cruelty was my weapon of choice, and I wielded it like a little boy who had found his daddy's gun. I loved the sensation of people under my heel, knowing I was in control of them. Maybe it was because of how Uncle Effram treated me and others, as well as my experiences with how people interacted with him because of it. He cheerfully lorded power over them, and he wasn't shy about letting them know where they stood in the pecking order. Usually, he would put people in their place with some backhanded compliment or passive aggressive poke. However, unlike Uncle Effram, I was far more lethal with my power.

I used it to get what I wanted, when I wanted it, and to bend people to my will.

I remember the first time I truly realized the extent of my influence.

I was down in the wine cellar looking for a bottle and putting some other stray bottles away when I heard a high-pitched, whiney voice calling down the stairs to me. "Looooooooooogaaaaaan, did you find the cabernet I like?"

I didn't respond. It's my wine cellar; of course, I found the cabernet she liked. It was a miserable, new-age number with no history, age, or taste whatsoever. It was basically Boones Farm for rich assholes. The only reason I had it was for moments like this.

"*LOOOOOOOOGAAAAAAAAAAAANNN...!*"

I responded in a low, edgy tone, "I have it."

"HUH!?"

Slightly louder, "I have it."

"Ohh, good!! Grab it and get your ass back up here; I'm horny again!"

I wiped the thin layer of dust away from the bottle label and thought to myself, Brittany was stupid, gorgeous, rich, and built for any inhuman sex act I could dream up. She was perfect...for tonight. However, tomorrow night, I would need a woman with those attributes who could offer me an intelligent conversation. Hearing Brittany try to wax intellectual about anything was painful.

Maybe Colleen? She was brilliant and absolutely beautiful, even if she was always complaining about my eating red meat - which was basically all I ate.

Or maybe Jessica, but she barely spoke any English. She was more of a Thursday night thing anyway. Then there was Monica 4 - God, I needed to stop dating Monicas - but she was too clingy.

"*LOOOOOOOOGAAAAAAAAAAAANNN...*!" Brittany cried out for a third time.

"I'm coming," I said curtly.

"You will be soon!" She said in a high, bubbly, irritatingly cheery voice. "Just get the hell up here and fuck me already! Don't forget the wine!"

I rolled my eyes and groaned. I picked the cab up off the tasting table and had a thought. "Why don't you come down here?" I was going to fuck her on the uncomfortable wine tasting table. I knew she would do whatever I wanted.

I could hear her moan as she descended the stairs, "You better be naked when I get down there."

I was. The first thing to appear on the stairs were the frilly little slippers that I kept in a box marked Brittany; then, I saw a nice long stretch of perfect legs.

Brittany appeared in full view and was also completely naked. "It's chilly down here!" She shivered and hugged herself tightly.

"Come here." She instantly obeyed.

"Ohhhhh, baby!" She scuttled over to me and put her arms around my neck. "You gonna show me how much you love me right here on the table," she said in a foxy, low tone.

"I'm going to show you how much I don't love you," I said in a smoldering baritone.

"Even better!" She giggled.

I couldn't help but roll my eyes again as our lips met, and I closed my hands over her firm breasts. She garishly began moaning and breathing heavily as my hands explored the rest of her body.

She entangled herself in my arms and forcefully pressed her mound against my cock. I was in the moment now and began lightly biting her nipples and fondling her clit, which escalated her breathing to a series of gasps.

Making sure to keep the routine fresh, I spread her legs with my thighs and pressed her forcefully up against the wall. I was powerful but tender and rubbed my rising dick against her clit until I was truly hard.

She kept her arms around my neck and hoisted herself up to straddle me. Using the wall as leverage, she pressed her pussy against my cock, but wouldn't let me inside just yet. She rode me vertically this way until we were both soaked. I had to hand it to her, she knew her way around a dick, even if she didn't know her way around a conversation.

Gritting my teeth, I put my hands underneath her arms, picked her up and brought her down roughly, forcing myself inside her! She screamed and came instantly, squirting her cum all over me. I gave her no reprieve and continued to punish her with pleasure.

She began to convulse, so I released her and guided her over to the tasting table. I laid her back down on the rough oak wood without a word and buried my face in her. I loved the way she tasted, and I let her know it. She grabbed my hair with both hands and drove my tongue deeper inside.

As I savored her, she arched her back and climaxed directly into my mouth.

"OhmyGod, fuck me!" She cried out.

Instead, I continued going down on her until I was sure she was about to cum again; only then did I slide my cock slowly into her. She began spasming and crying out, but I still didn't let up!

I climbed on top of her and the table, slipped my muscular arms underneath her, and thrust myself in and out of her with measured pressure. She met my movements with her own and gave in to the mercy of multiple orgasms.

I was a generous lover, so I pulled out and went down on her again! She grabbed the back of her knees and raised her inner thighs to grant me more entry with my skilled tongue. Like an animal, I devoured her and thought nothing of the world around us.

She came again, then rolled over onto her knees and begged me to fuck her from behind. Needing no invitation, I mounted her and eased slowly into a rhythm.

This was one of my favorite positions; classic but effective. I knew I would cum explosively very soon, so I kept the pressure on. I leaned in to kiss the back of her neck as she found my tempo. We began undulating in unison, and both of us hit the crescendo simultaneously! I withdrew and decorated her back in pearly flowers.

Exhausted, we collapsed into each other's arms, spent and sweat covered. I laid on my back, with her on my chest, as she purred sweet nothings into my ear like a kitten.

I gathered my strength, pulled myself off the table, and grabbed a real bottle of wine off the rack. I popped the cork and smelled the intoxicating fragrance.

"Is that the cab I like?" Brittany asked from a place close to sleep.

"No. I have an early meeting tomorrow morning, so..."

"Asshole."

I spoke as little as possible. I rarely had to; I preferred a look. I certainly didn't speak much when I was growing up with Uncle Effram, and I soon learned that speaking with others was typically a waste of time. Some people appreciated my silence, most didn't; eventually, they feared it because it meant my gears were turning.

My silence made me a target in school and university because people presumed I was crazy. Nevertheless, at boarding school, when I used pliers to pull the pinky fingernail from a particularly menacing bully while he slept, people quickly steered clear of my bad side. I never faced punishment for the deed either because all the students were too terrified of me to report it. Former classmates who followed me to university made sure my reputation as a calculating and callus bastard with a capacity for revenge followed me as well. Most people thankfully left me to my own devices. This was another big lesson for me. Using fear as a tool of dominance was my second greatest talent and my most powerful weapon.

In the past, my appearance, physically and perceptually, meant absolutely *everything* to me. I was consumed with my physique, hair, teeth, complexion, nails, scent, and wardrobe. I was a beautiful man on the outside, but on the inside, I was a monster. Naturally, my fixation transcended personal image. Soon, I had to have the biggest, most beautiful, contemporary mansion with all the latest amenities; I had to have the nicest, shiniest, most expensive cars; and my friends could only come from esteemed, wealthy, and elite families. Every thread, every stitch within the tapestry of my life, had to fit snugly within the weave of superiority.

Vanity ruled my world, much to the detriment of health and true happiness. I would lay awake at night, still as a tombstone but inwardly toiling over my ideas of other people's shrewd intuition. I would endlessly analyze things I had said, things that were said to me, subtle looks, gestures - body language. Under the microscope was every molecule and atom of my life, begging to be poured over and milled for the slightest hint of fatalistic judgment from others. If I felt it came from someone beneath me, I crushed them relentlessly; if it came from someone of stature, I stopped at nothing to prove my worth, and then I crushed them relentlessly. Nothing was more important to me than being held in high esteem or envied. Everyone had to be equal in their jealous admiration of me.

The fact that I was so captivated by others' impressions, wealthy or otherwise, was simultaneously my greatest strength, and my most profound weakness. Such attention to others' perceptions was a grand motivator! It helped me overcome many obstacles and achieve goals others might believe never possible. It made me strong, confident, tenacious, and unyielding. It gave me the strength to pursue art, obtain vast wealth, and rise like the sun in my world.

Conversely, the other side of the razor forced me to measure my worth by the yardage of others.

It placed ridiculous expectations for happiness upon the unwitting shoulders of every individual on Earth. I could never live up to my own expectations, viewed through the lens of others.

There was one topic in my life that, above all else, called down my wrath if mentioned, or even hinted at. It was entirely beyond my control or ability to overcome despite all my wealth and attributes. Origin. I had no legacy. I came from nothing. I had no family name. I had no regal bloodline to lift me up. It was, at one time, my grandest shame.

The first and last time anyone ever dared mention my childhood and Uncle Effram, was at an art auction in New York, six years prior to the present. A very handsome, ruthless, highly reputable art critic for "Apex Art Magazine" named John Sellecky made the disastrous mistake of openly confronting me about my tumultuous beginnings in a room full of my peers. Everyone gasped and gawked in anticipation of my response because they all knew how taboo the subject was to me.

I quietly, slowly, sashayed up to him and, never saying a word, stared him dead in the eyes for a very long, awkward moment. John feigned strength and indifference, but I knew he was rattled. I put both of my hands on either side of his head, reeled him in, and kissed him deeply on the lips. He was stunned, so he made no effort to stop me.

I caressed my hands lovingly down his face, neck, and arms to his hands and took them up inside my own. Up to this point, I had only been seen romantically involved with gorgeous, esteemed women of wealth and power, so this escapade proffered me many shocked faces.

I held John's hands for another eternity before leading him upstairs to the offices. Not that I have any issues with it personally, but I am not, nor have I ever been gay.

John was also, to my knowledge, straight as an arrow. Nevertheless, I took him to the back offices without speaking, slowly undressed him, and fucked him like a 16th Century whore.

Over the next six months, I made him love me. I made him love me more than he had ever loved anything. I pampered him. I whispered lovingly to him every night. I made him promises. I made commitments to him. I introduced him to people he would have never known otherwise. I arranged interviews with the art world's most influential talents. I elevated him to such a lofty pinnacle, so when he fell from that great height, it would be absolutely devastating.

And fall from a great height he did. It was during a hotly anticipated television and publication interview with world-renowned art reporter Adrian Seerlie of "The Global Arts Publication," when I finally dropped the hammer.

John was with me; I had asked Seerlie if we could touch on my relationship and how it affected my art and inspiration. He was more than happy to oblige, thinking it would make for a spicy and fascinating interview. He wasn't wrong about that, but I ultimately blindsided him with how it would be a spicy and fascinating interview.

When the topic of our relationship came up, John excitedly squeezed my hand. You see, I had attributed most of my inspiration to him in the late hours of the night after sex. One of my many false promises was that I would soon publicly proclaim him my muse and the reason my most recent work had evolved so dramatically.

Seerlie interviewed John briefly and unwittingly set him up for the grand plunge. John went on and on about how much he loved me, about how he never thought he would love a man the way he loved me; and about how his entire life had changed for the better after becoming my inspiration.

When Seerlie brought the interview back around to me and how we met, I pulled my hand away from John's and laughed. The shock was tattooed on both of their faces, and I drank it like fine wine.

"Let me tell you about the first time we met, Seerlie. The first time I met John, he profoundly insulted me in front of everyone I know and respect. He came to the Manhattan Art Auction with the sole intent of humiliating me. Isn't that right, John?"

John was flabbergasted. He didn't know where this was coming from or where I was going with it. His uncertainty and fear were intoxicating. Trying to defuse the situation, John nervously laughed and said, "That's not entirely true! I wanted to ask you some tough questions in order to make my article more intriguing. You can understand that, right Seerlie!?"

Seerlie pensively giggled, "I sure can!"

John continued, "Then you kissed me without a word, and I knew right away that you were the one." John blushed sweetly at the memory. "I wasn't even out of the closet yet at the time! Hell, I didn't even realize I was in," John joked. "In fact -" John began, but I cut him off curtly.

"God, you are so *fucking* pathetic," I stated flatly. Faces instantly changed all at once around the room. John, Seerlie, the staff - the fucking caterer - all gasped in awkward dismay.

"You publicly shamed me, and you know it. You relished the idea of someone like you kneecapping someone like me. I spoke to the magazine's director the very next day and squeeeeeeezed the truth out of him about your true intentions surrounding the article," I snapped.

"Something about how you intended to shine a very bright light on my childhood misfortune and twist the past around to hurt me. You had every intention of seeing that through to fruition. Didn't you?"

John stuttered and fretfully tried to conjure words, but he was bleeding out and dazed. "N...no...of course not!"

"Horseshit!" I hissed! "If I hadn't kissed you, If I hadn't acted immediately the way I had, you would have run that trash article and endeavored to paint the painter in a very unflattering medium, am I right!? Not only are you a sneak-thief, you're a coward and a liar too!"

John's words and tears came simultaneously, "How could you!? You're the liar! You fabricated such poisonous falsehoods over the past six months! You're the Devil! You told me you loved me, that I was your muse! That we would always be together!"

"Poor, John. Playing the victim is the last bastion of a coward. You expect me to feel pity for you!? Clearly, you can dish it out, but you can't take it. I've read your previous garbage articles, and you take great joy in dragging others through the deepest, darkest mud you can dredge up. Well, now I am simply returning the favor. The idea that I could love an insufferably needy, sniveling, spineless heel like you is laughable," I snarled.

"Seerlie, this dashingly handsome, dearly confused man, was at his core, a conniving, weak and wanton fool. I'm sure scores of people from prior articles would agree with me there. Now you try to play the sufferer!? Shame on you. Take this pain, this pain you've foisted on others, this pain you intended for me, and own it. The time you have enjoyed in the art world is over, my friend! No one will talk to you from here on out. Go now."

John ran from the room, pouring tears from his swollen eyes. Seerlie, like all the rest, wore a face of pure and total disbelief. "Well...that was unexpected," Seerlie managed to croak out.

"I apologize for the unpleasantness, Seerlie. If you would like to ask me *any* questions about my sexuality, childhood, or past, I will gladly answer...and never take issue."

"I'm absolutely honored - and terrified - to ask," Seerlie confessed.

I checked - and I'm happy to address it now. Your talent as an art journalist is second to none, and I very much respect you. That said, I trust I will never, ever, *EVER* have to discuss this again with anyone. And, you can quote me on this: I will salt the earth under the feet of anyone daring to bring this subject up again."

"Wow. Okay. So, where to begin? Are you gay?" Seerlie managed.

"Not exclusively," I quipped. "Next question..."

It took a few days before I heard from Seerlie; I presumed he was waiting to see how the interview landed with the public. As I anticipated, it was his most watched, read and discussed interview in the long history of his career.

Additionally, my stunt garnered the highest ratings of any art related interview - ever. Finally, the magazine sold out in pre-order, which is absolutely unheard of.

Not only that, but there was an outpouring of support for me from the art community and beyond. Everyone loved how I "Cruella de Vil-ed" my now publicly despised former lover.

It was all anyone in the entertainment or art industries could talk about for a very long time. Naturally, there were others who tried to ape my epic on-air bitch slap, but all were considered pale by comparison.

Last I heard, John was living alone in South Carolina, working as a mason. The person I was then was so pleased with himself that it made the person I am now sick to my stomach with guilt and regret. To know I was once capable of such callousness haunted me.

To this day, I find it incredibly surprising that my public humiliation of John was not the circumstance to foist me from my pedestal.

Chapter Two

The Condition

Logan

Courtney licked her dry lips to moisten them after half an hour of gasping and pleading. I didn't let up. I eagerly devoured her. I didn't love her, but I loved that she loved me. She encouraged me gently with soft hands to join her above the sheets in a rugged kiss. I shared her taste as she guided me between her legs.

A rhythm found us, and I let her take control. Courtney was beautiful and emotionally resonant, as well as carefree and impetuous. I might have been able to genuinely love her, had I not been such a void.

Courtney was an incredible lover because she knew that men - all men - validated themselves through sex. She was well aware of that flaw in our DNA and used the knowledge to her benefit. I say this with admiration, not malice, mind you.

Not only did she glide lasciviously up and down on top of me in a calculated and thoughtful way, but she also whispered such lovely affirmations in my ear with honey in her voice. We were both using each other for different reasons, and our symbiotic relationship made for sumptuous lovemaking.

My crushing, hidden insecurities vanished when I was tangled up in her, which was far more satisfying than any climax. It was the feeling of weightlessness I experienced when I was with her that was truly poignant. That said, her beauty, body, and fearlessness never left me wanting.

I knew she was close to cumming when she began slowly rising up to the very edge and then plunging down hard and desperately. There was repetition but also imagination in her final movements that sent us both soaring over the precipice.

"I love you," she said breathlessly as she fell off me and to the side. She ran her fingers lovingly over my face but hesitated. "What's this?" Courtney caressed a small, raised, barely visible, pea-sized lump beneath my right eye. "You should get that checked out."

You ugly, disgusting, miserable, subhuman conglomerate of rebellious cells, I think to the reflection in the mirror that has betrayed me. My body politic is one of comeuppance and retribution. I can no longer speak, so this has become my internal mantra - my silent gospel.

Locked in a prison of my own treacherous flesh, my heart knows no bottom to the abyss. I cannot stop thinking obsessively...I deserve this.

The condition is called Neurofibromatosis Type 2. It typically manifests in early adulthood; mine happened to develop a little later in my life. My doctor seemed surprised that the condition hadn't presented itself until now but suspected it had been lurking for some time. It started out as round protruding patches that became large, fibrous lipomas or tumors that quickly enveloped my face.

Mine was benign, but even after surgery, chemo, and medication, they came back; my inner ugliness manifesting itself in the meat of my appearance, I suppose. Since Courtney discovered my condition in the summer of 2013, a significant portion of my lower face has been enveloped in porous lipomas. I get them removed and treat them when they become too painful or compromise my breathing and sight. I typically don't speak because the tumors invade my mouth, making it difficult. For that reason, I learned sign language.

This was the circumstance that foisted me from my pedestal.

"I...I don't know what to say, Logan. I truly am sorry," Courtney spoke through a mouthful of mournful and wayward tears.

"I understand," I managed through a mouthful of melanoma and bitterness. "Honestly, I didn't expect you to stay with me this long. Thank you for everything." I wasn't sad; I wasn't mad; I completely understood why she had to leave. "Go. Just go. It's okay. Really, I'd leave me too."

Courtney, genuinely heartbroken, solemnly lifted her purse to her chest and left. She was the last of my circle to depart, and I would never see her again.

I looked around with my left eye at the hushed, seven million dollar penthouse in Central Park South, New York, and tried to grasp my situation.

I had lost everyone I thought I knew at the age of 40.

At first, all the people in my life were attentive and ostentatiously supportive. They promised me I could overcome this. They assured me that no matter what, I would never be alone. But, as the condition languished, one by one, they all vanished from my life in one way or another.

The first person to desert me was my agent, Matilda. I always respected her merciless nature when it came to business until she turned that mercilessness on me like a predator. Pretty soon after the diagnosis, my new face began to show itself, so Matilda showed me her teeth.

Matilda let it leak to the press that I was terminally ill with months to live, massively drove up the price on all of my existing work, sold everything for triple the cost, fucked me on the commission, and then dropped me like a bag of horseshit. She severed our contract in breach, paid me a paltry million dollars, but made $50 million on the backend. I had to respect her shrewdness. She candidly told me, over the phone - no less - that no one would fault her for dropping me as a client, and she would be right.

The departure continued with my acquaintances and "friends." It was so gradual that the abandonment was almost imperceptible. I suppose having an outwardly disfigured friend is somehow far worse than having an emotionally disfigured friend. It says a lot about the world we live in.

Everyone had rallied around me when I ate John alive on national television, but now that I was deformed, sick and weak, they all wanted to euthanize me.

I, much like John, disappeared into obscurity shortly after my condition had worsened and moved to nowhere New Jersey within the year. I've lived in a nice Victorian house in Cape May for the past five years, but it may as well have been a prison. I now wore a silky black hood with eye-holes like a Bond villain whenever I went out or had to interact with people; I was also a fat, depressed and self-deprecating mess, thanks to the depression surrounding my condition, and the subsequent realization that I was an awful person.

I had managed to retain my wealth and vast investments, thanks to my accountant and only remaining friend, Wilma.

"Still wearing the mysterious hood, I see. Might be a little overkill for the pandemic, but certainly apropos. You may not be traditionally handsome any longer, my dear boy, but you are still rich, so there is hope for you yet. You're welcome, by the way," Wilma, my seasoned and sexy sixty-year-old accountant, said flatly behind a smoldering cigar and scotch on the rocks during our 8am Zoom meeting. Her sprawling, awe-inspiring office, drenched in cherry wood, was the perfect backdrop for her. "I guess all that money and this Covid pandemic is working well for a wealthy, hooded recluse like yourself?"

I raised my hands to respond in sign language, "Everyone can now taste the exquisite flavor of my life."

Wilma formed a knowing and friendly frown, "Even in silence you speak so eloquently."

"You flatter me," I motioned. "I guess this pandemic is working nicely for you as well," I signed. "Now you can smoke your cigars during work and conference meetings all you like!"

"Silver linings," Wilma said gruffly. "How are you, Logan? Seriously, Ted and I worry about you being cooped up all alone like this for so long."

"I was cooped up all alone for years before the pandemic, so..."

"Yes, well, the longer you stay cooped up, the more I worry about you."

I shrugged it off. The new me was the old me, minus the handsome face, swagger, and confidence. Using only my right hand, I gestured, "Stop."

"Alright, Logan. I'll stop, but you should really consider getting out and getting laid," she snickered.

At this, I shook my head "yes" and raised my middle finger.

Wilma laughed a deep and throaty laugh, "Well, I suppose I had that coming. Glad I learned sign language only to have you flip me off. You have a good morning, Logan, and I'll come by to see you soon. Please be sure to have the good scotch on hand."

I slowly nodded my head and waved goodbye. Wilma smiled a very genuine and gracious smile and waved goodbye as well.

Without warning, my doorbell rang!

Chapter Three

Breakfast with Strangers

Logan

I stared at the front door like it had six heads. What the fuck? I didn't even realize I had a doorbell. Had I known, I would have had it removed. DING DONG! It rang loudly again. I'll just wait until they go away. DING DONG! Shouldn't be much longer now. DING DONG! Jesus, Mary and fucking Joseph, who the Hell- DING DONG! Fuck sake! DING DONG!

I fumbled with my hood, trying to get it over my head before answering the door. It was more to hide my face than prevent Covid, but I still couldn't manage to get it on. DING DONG! Seething, I threw the hood aside, stormed over to the front door in all my deformed glory, and ripped it open!

There, standing like a lone daisy in a field, was the most beautiful, 35ish woman I had ever seen. She had long flowing dirty blonde locks, a black eye, and a samurai sword. She was wearing nothing but panties, an oversized plaid shirt - barely buttoned - no bra, and combat boots.

If I had been able to talk, I would have been speechless. She looked me dead in the eyes, tilted her head a bit at my face, and without missing a beat said, "My name is Tess, and if you don't let me in, I'm going to stab you."

I stood there for a moment, bewildered. "Well...?" She asked impatiently. I pulled the door open all the way, bowed and motioned for her to come in with a sweep of my arm. "Thanks," she managed curtly. I closed the door, turned around, and drank her in.

The juxtaposition of a lovely, slender, disheveled pixie holding such an impressive weapon of death intrigued me.

"So, uh, yeah, not gonna stab you, but I didn't have time to risk a long explanation," Tess said, buttoning up her shirt.

DING DONG! "Fuuuuuck!" she whispered and shouted simultaneously. Her eyes brimmed with burgeoning tears that pleaded with me. I held out my hand and softly motioned for her to relax. DING DONG! I snatched up my hood and managed to get it over my head this time while Tess ducked into the guest bathroom down the hall. I slowly opened the door...

There on my porch stood a 30 something, statuesque, gorgeous black woman, dressed as an action movie villain, with a matching black, fancy Covid facemask that had cartoon lips on it. With her was a very muscular black man, in nothing but shorts and a plain medical Covid facemask. There beside him were two of the cutest fraternal twins I have ever laid eyes on. The kids couldn't have been older than 6 and were dressed in matching Covid face masks and clothes.

The woman spoke respectfully and frankly, "Hello there. My name is Natish; you must be Cobra Commander. Interesting facemask. Annnywho, I saw that lady make her way to your door, and I can only assume she forced you to let her in with my husband's sword?"

I motioned with my hand that I was unable to speak. "I understand," she said. "I realize how all this must look; suffice it to say, an explanation is in order. After that, maybe you can explain that creepy ass hood to me."

I reached over to a side table, picked up a pad and pen, and wrote, "Explanations all around! My name is Logan. Disabled and deformed."

Natish and her husband read my note and nodded. "Logan. That's one of my favorite names. This is my husband, Furious, named after Lawrence Fishburne in 'Boyz 'n the Hood.'" Furious politely waved. "These two beautiful babies are our children, Nina and Jamal," both of whom politely waved as well. "We aren't looking for any trouble. That...-*woman* has been squatting in our vacation home down the road, and I guess we surprised her when we showed up. She was asleep upstairs when my husband went to change his clothes and startled her awake. She grabbed his special edition Platinum handled, "Kill Bill" Hattori Hanzo replica sword - signed by Sonny Chiba, Uma Thurman, and Quentin Tarantino - and started waving it in our faces."

Natish sighed and continued, "We don't care about the squatting; we just want our sword back. It's worth a lot and holds a great deal of sentimental value."

I put my head around the situation for a brief moment and wrote, "Of course. She is here; let me try to PEACEFULLY get your sword back."

"That would be ideal," Natish said calmly. "Tell her sorry for the black eye, but uninvited strangers in my home, waving samurai swords, get they ass smacked."

I nodded my head but couldn't help snickering a bit. I instantly liked Natish.

Before I even made it to the guest bathroom, Tess sheepishly appeared in the hall and started slowly walking into the living room. "I'm really sorry about all this, you guys. I'm so embarrassed. There's a whole sob story, which I'll spare you, but here's your sword. You guys just startled me, is all."

Natish stepped through the threshold of my house like a Boss, hand outstretched, "I can relate. No harm." Tess courteously handed over the Kitana to Natish handle first, who calmly took it and handed it to her husband. "You know if you're in some kind of trouble, maybe I can help?"

With that, Tess broke down into tears and crumpled to the ground sobbing. Natish looked at me, but all I could do was shrug. "Okay, girl. Hold it together." Natish turned to Furious, "Honey, would you mind taking the kids home and getting them some breakfast? I'll be there shortly to help you unpack. I'll take..."

"Tess," I wrote on the pad and showed it to her.

"...Tess to get something to eat and try to figure this mess out. That is, of course, unless Logan here wouldn't mind helping a couple ladies out with a talk space and some waffles." Natish looked at me with eyes that sweetly demanded more than asked.

"I know that look, bro. She's dead serious. Betta get those waffles goin'," Furious said with a snicker. "I'll get the kids some breakfast, baby. You do your thing." Furious gave Natish a loving kiss. "Nice to meet you, Logan."

Out of habit, I signed, "Nice to meet you too." Furious smiled, understanding the sentiment more than the signs, and led the kids away.

Nina and Jamal both looked over their shoulders and called out, "Nice to meet you, Logan!"

I put my hand over my heart and nodded. Sooooo cute!

"You better be careful walking through this neighborhood being black, half-dressed, with a samurai sword!" Natish called out to Furious as he escorted Nina and Jamal back toward their house.

"E'rbody knows who I am around here!" he said and then began to sing loudly, "I'm FUUUUURIOUS!"

Natish giggled and looked back at me with patient eyes, so I extended my hand and invited her in. I've lived here five years without so much as a peep from anyone, and now all this. It was actually kind of nice to have company after so long, no matter how unusual the circumstances were.

Natish looked at me, "Now you nodded your head, so I assume that means you have waffles, and if you got waffles, you got butter, syrup, and coffee, right?"

I nodded my head, "yes," again.

"Excellent," she said. "Have you both been vaccinated?"

I nodded, and Tess sobbed out a "yes."

Natish took her mask off. "Good. Me too. Now take that ridiculous hood off, go get this girl some pants, and make us some breakfast - *please*! I'll get Tess here straightened out," she said while tenderly helping Tess up.

Acquiescing to the situation, I pulled my hood off, bowed my head shyly, and turned away toward the kitchen. I missed being outwardly handsome; it always commanded respect and often placed me in a position of strength.

Natish reached out and lightly grabbed my arm. She leaned in, looked me in the eyes, and said, "Thank you, Logan. You're very kind." Kind? If she only knew.

"Thanks, Logan," Tess sniffled from the floor and hiccuped. "Sorry about the...threat to your life." I timidly nodded my head again and went into the kitchen. I instantly liked Tess as well.

As I put breakfast together, I reflected on the situation. I'm pretty sure the old me would have slammed the door in their faces and called the cops.

I guess I was changing on the inside as well as the outside. It would seem my personality and physical appearance were swapping places. My heart smiled inwardly at the thought, but quick as a shot came to the reality of what a miserable bastard I had been most of my life, and my heart sank again.

I inconspicuously listened in on the conversation between Natish and Tess and was able to gather a substantial amount of information about the circumstances that led everyone to my front door. Apparently, Tess, 34, had lost her job as a sous-chef in an upscale New York restaurant due to the pandemic, had used up all her money, had no real friends, absolutely no family, and was an aspiring chef. She had followed her boyfriend of two months, Bryce - yeah, Bryce - to the Cape after losing her job. He had promised her a sous chef position at his father's restaurant. Turns out he was lying about everything. There was no father, no job, and no restaurant. Evidently, his plan was to try and get her hooked on methamphetamine so he could pimp her out. Nice fella.

The moment meth entered the picture, she tried to leave. Bryce, it seemed, wasn't having it. He tried to abduct her and forcibly inject her with the highly addictive drug, but she had managed to get away.

She slept on the streets for a few weeks until she was certain Natish's house was empty. She disabled the power to deactivate the alarm system and had been living there for the last three days, trying to get herself together. Pretty harrowing story.

I caught my previous self trying to sneak in and think her a ne'er do well, but I pushed the thought away and committed myself to not fall into old ways of thinking. Besides, Tess was really growing on me; no pun intended.

I brought a tray with a carafe of French-pressed coffee, 3 cups, sugar and creme into the living room for my new guests. They eagerly poured a cup, added their preferences, and drank up. I joined them, and I needed it.

"Ohmygawd, I needed that!" Tess said, reading my mind. She was now wearing a pair of my older pants, back from when I was thin, but they still swallowed her whole. Her eyes were as swollen as a professional fighter, but she seemed to be getting it together. Natish wiped away a single tear but still looked as polished as an hour ago.

I held up a small dry erase board from my office that read: "Waffles and bacon in the dining room."

Natish smiled from ear to ear, "I forgot to ask if you had any bacon, and here you are with bacon. You, sir, are my hero."

"I couldn't agree more," Tess said between huge gulps of coffee.

I extended my hand towards the dining room.

As we sat and ate, the two ladies chatted like old pals. I endeavored not to slurp and chew noisily; my condition made it slightly challenging, but I managed.

Natish looked over my head for a long moment, and I suddenly realized she was studying one of my older paintings.

"Hoooooolllyyyyyy shit. Logan. Logan Lepozod!" Natish proclaimed! "Tell me that's you!"

I bashfully nodded "yes", and she slapped the table with both hands.

"Oh. My. God! I can't believe it! My husband and I are HUGE fans!" She was gushing. "We bought three of your paintings! I have *Mackenzie's Ukulele*, *Scar Tissue*, and *Disgusting Faced*!"

I held both hands over my heart to illustrate my genuine gratitude. *Mackenzie's Ukulele* sold for six hundred thousand dollars almost 8 years ago, I presumed to Natish.

The other two I painted from a very dark place after Matilda unceremoniously fucked me. They sold for next to nothing when it became public knowledge that I wasn't terminal. In fact, they were among the last 5 pieces I ever sold. I tilted my head for a moment, then wrote on my dry erase board, "Natalie Sultz?"

"That's me, baby!" Natish was overcome with emotion. "You are, without a doubt, my - and my husband's - favorite artist! I would have so much more of your work if we could afford it!"

I wrote on my board, "I'll give you a deal on anything I have here! Most of my older work is no longer my work, though, so...Thank you for buying my newer stuff; it wasn't selling so well."

"Are you kidding me!? I found it to be some of your most poignant - and affordable work! I would have bought the remaining three of your last series, but someone else beat me to the punch. I was always so thankful I got the two. They were my favorites anyway."

"It's kind of weird; I know a lot about you," she admitted. "I hope I'm not being too forward when I say it was inspirational the way you worked through your...condition by painting. Very brave."

I paused for a long moment and wrote, "I'm not so sure I worked through it very well. As you can see, I'm a recluse, which makes me the furthest thing from 'brave'."

"You're sticking it out, honey, and that's brave. Certainly these days," Natish said matter of factly.

Lightening the mood and pointing to the painting behind me, Tess suddenly chimed in, "I'll be damned! The restaurant I worked at in New York had a print of that hanging in the foyer! The head chef said they couldn't get the original, and now I know why! You're an absolutely incredible talent!"

I shook my head and jotted on the board, "You two are going to make me blush! Not that you could tell on this face," I finished writing and added a little smiley face after.

"Don't do that," Tess said quietly. "Don't make jokes about how you look. It's irrelevant. You opened your door to complete strangers, one in desperate need, gave us a place to talk, and even made us a magnificent breakfast. That's beautiful. That makes you beautiful." She gave me a shy smile and looked directly into my eyes.

The words hit me like a ton of bricks. I was so taken aback, I couldn't stop blinking. I didn't know what to do. I took a moment, cleared my throat and mind, and wrote on the board, "Thank you. That's the nicest thing anyone has ever said to me, but how do you know I'm not a horrible bastard? More coffee?"

"A horrible bastard would have slammed the door in our faces and called the cops," Tess stated.

I chuckled and went to get more coffee. Indeed, that's exactly what a horrible bastard would have done.

As we wrapped up breakfast, Natish stepped out onto the porch for a smoke and a chat with her hubby on her cell phone. Tess helped me with washing and drying the dishes. While we've only known each other for about 3 hours, we had a cadence and tempo. Tess was refreshingly intuitive and anticipated what needed to be done, probably from her years of working in a kitchen. She finished drying the dishes, so I stepped out to the living room for a moment to collect myself.

This was all so foreign and sudden to me. I had taken myself out of the human equation for so long that I'd forgotten what the dynamic was like. Not to mention, in the past, I was more inhuman than human when I was a part of the human equation. I just didn't know where my place was anymore. I made sure not to get too comfortable with the idea that people are warm and fuzzy. There is always the possibility of pain where people are concerned.

Nevertheless, I really wanted to be brave here because I truly liked Tess and the Sultz family; they were so vastly different from the self-absorbed, spoiled trolls I had been used to cozying up with in the past. They seemed...real. There wasn't much more pain that could be heaped upon me at this point, so I figured making friends was worth the risk. Chances were very good they would soon walk out his door, as well as his life forever, and things would go right back to the way they were.

Out of fear, I had initially wanted them to disappear from my life, but now I found myself hoping they would stay. They seemed like actual people, with blood flowing through their veins, not smarmy, frosty aristocrats who were always looking for a weakness to exploit. I should know, I was one of those aristocrats; these people made me want to be different from the old me in every way.

Tess. So beautiful and so damaged. The combination was irresistible to me. Damage seeks damage, I guess. Maybe I could offer her a place to stay until she gets back on her feet? The idea of someone else sharing my space was simultaneously exhilarating and terrifying.

It could work, though! I mean, I had three guest rooms, three full bathrooms and a ton of space. Not to mention plenty of money to help her get back on track. I decided I would ask her to stay until she was stable enough to leave. In any case, I was suddenly overcome with excitement over the possibility of some companionship in my sprawling, cold, lonely house. A real friend. Not a friend born of false pretense, which was typical of my former circle. Someone who didn't seem to care one bit about my past or present condition.

Just friends. No sexual tension, no hidden agendas, no secrets - just two people helping each other out! I had made up my mind.

Natish came back in through the front door like she had lived here for years. She confidently walked up to me and put her right hand on my left shoulder," Where is Tess? I spoke to Furious, and he said it was okay if she stayed with us until she gets back on her feet. I think a solid family dynamic may be just what she needs."

Of course, that's a better idea. Jesus, I didn't know what I was thinking! I was inwardly kicking myself for being such a fool. I'd be lying if I said I wasn't profoundly disappointed, but the arrangement made so much more sense. Had I become so obtuse in my solitude?

Natish read the disappointment in my eyes, "We are truly lucky to have crashed into you, Logan. Any other stuffed up, rich, spoiled piece of shit in this community would have had a S.W.A.T. team down here immediately to lock up the homeless vagrant and harass the black family running around here without country club passes."

"You are now a dear friend of the Sultz family, and we will *NEVER* let you forget it!" She loudly guffawed, and it sang to me. "I pride myself on being a good judge of character, and I really like you two. That...doesn't happen often. Certainly not with a couple 'a crackers!" She burst out laughing again, and I couldn't help but join her. That was the first time I really laughed in - forever. I honestly don't think I have ever sincerely laughed.

Out of habit, I signed with my hands that I really liked her too. She shook her head, "I'm assuming that means you love my ass."

I laughed again and nodded enthusiastically, "Yes."

"Well then, I expect you to come over for dinner this weekend at our house, so I can repay your kindness! We're number 208 Jackson Street! I hope you like BBQ!" I emphatically nodded yes, but was pretty sure I had never eaten BBQ in my life. "There's going to be a lot of people there, all vaccinated, but if it's a problem, I completely understand."

I waved it off for the moment but knew I'd have to face the fear and uncertainty of a BBQ with lots of people very soon.

Tess came out of the kitchen, drying her hands with a dishrag. "Stop telling secrets, you two!"

Natish took the dishrag from Tess and held her hands, "Honey, there ain't no secrets in my world! So, I talked to Furious, and we'd like to invite you to stay with us until you can get on solid ground again."

"Oh, I couldn't impose on you and your family like that! That's really thoughtful and kind, but I just wouldn't feel right about it," Tess confessed. "I have some friends in New York I can stay with for a while. I have enough money to ride the train up there. I'll be okay, really!"

"Stop lyin' to me! I know you ain't got any friends as good as Logan and me," she said, winking at me. "It's not an imposition; you already know your way around the house!" she added, chuckling. "So stop trying to be polite, shut the fuck up, and do me the honor of helping a sister out."

Tess thought on it for a minute, but I could tell she was very conflicted about putting Natish out. "You're so kind, Natish. I feel like such a charity case."

"Girl, you need to stop talking like that. Just because someone needs a little help doesn't make them a charity case. You've had a rough time; I've been there." Natish proclaimed.

"I don't know..." Tess said quietly.

I held up my hand as if to say, "Wait a minute." They both looked at me quizzically. I started writing on the pad, trying not to seem too eager.

After a moment, I held up the note, "You can stay with me. I have plenty of room, no family, and I could actually use some help around here with things. If you run some errands, did some work for me, I'd be happy to pay you and let you stay here as long as you need. No charity, it's a job."

Tess looked at Natish; Natish thought about it for a minute and slowly nodded her head. "I mean, we're happy to have you, Tess, but my kids would probably drive you insane within an hour!"

We all laughed at that. "Well, if you're sure it's not a burden, and if you really do have work that needs to be done..." Tess said, rubbing her chin.

I wrote on my pad again, "Trust me, there's work. You said you're a chef, and I desperately need to go on a diet." As if to emphasize, I pinched my round stomach. Hard to believe I was once in great shape.

"Well...alright then!" Tess announced! "Wait, you're not some kind of weirdo serial killer, are you?"

I took a moment before nodding my head "yes," and shrugging my shoulders. Then I wrote on my pad, "How do I know you aren't a weirdo serial killer?!"

"Fair 'nuff," Tess admitted. "Don't kill me, and I won't kill you. Deal?"

I held out my hand, and she shook it.

"Well, now that's settled, I'll expect to see both of you on Saturday for our BBQ!" Natish slapped us both on the backs, "I like this! Oh, honey, I'll be by later with some clothes - we're about the same size - 'cause *this*," she held her hands up to frame Tess, "Ain't workin' for you."

We all laughed like old friends, and Natish sauntered out of the house. Tess and I looked at each other for an awkward moment. "Well, what now?" Tess asked.

I wrote on the pad, "Lunch?"

Chapter Four

Beau-laid

Tess

I sat on Logan's couch watching "Night of the Creeps," which was one of my all-time favorite horror movies. I absolutely loved scary movies! Everything from top-tier offerings like "The Shining" to independent horror titles like "The Good Things Devils Do"; all carried great worth in my eyes.

Logan pretended to do some work on his laptop in what I presumed was his favorite chair. He continued to wear his hood despite my telling him it wasn't necessary, saying "it was more for him than me." I completely understood where he was coming from, so I didn't pester him about it. Honestly, it was kind of mysterious.

I could tell my being there made Logan a little uncomfortable at first, but he quickly got used to me. I get the feeling he was starved for companionship. To tell the truth, so was I.

"You should get a dog," I blurted out of the blue, apparently reading his mind.

Startled, Logan typed into his type-to-voice app on the computer, "Get out of my head; It's scary in there! I love dogs!"

"Shit, try to spend a whole night in my head," I joked. "But you wanna talk about scary? hTat type-to-talk app is creepy as hell. Can you teach me sign language?"

Logan looked up from his computer and patted his leg.

"Leg?" I asked.

He chuckled and shook his head "no." Using the type-to-talk, he said, "Dog."

I nodded, "Okay, okay...What's the sign for...Tess?"

Logan thought for a moment, took his five fingers, placed them over his face, and brought them together at his chin.

"No kidding?! There's a sign for Tess?!"

He nodded his head. I would later learn this was the sign for beautiful.

"What's the sign for...Logan?" I asked.

Logan considered it, then pointed his index finger to one side of his face, underneath his nose, and quickly dragged it across in a ragged motion. And this sign, I would later discover, was the sign for ugly.

"That looks like the sign for mustache or dirty Sanchez," I joked. "Is that really the sign for you?"

Logan hesitated for a moment, nodded, and signed "yes" with his hand.

"Well, I don't like it," I said flatly. "What's the sign for sweet?"

He shook his head, hesitated, put his first two fingers to his chin, and reluctantly beckoned them down twice. He quickly typed into the computer, "I may seem sweet having known me for 12 hours, but give it a week, and we'll revisit the subject," the computer said robotically as he chuckled.

I sighed and tilted my head like I often did. "I think that's long enough, Logan," I said, saying Logan while signing sweet. "I don't know why you're so down on yourself, but you fed me, gave me a job, and a place to stay, so you're doing 'sweet' pretty well in my book."

"Just don't make me a permanent addition to your human doll collection or whatever, and we're good," I snickered, half joking and half serious.

Logan typed into his computer, and the chilling, emotionless voice spoke back, "But my collection is missing a Mommy."

"Like I said, creepy as fuck." We both burst out laughing.

It had only been four days, but by Friday, Logan and I were getting along really well! We had shared many stories about each other and our lives. to the point that we felt like old friends. I was pretty sure there were several things about his past that he was leaving out, but there was plenty I was leaving out as well. In any case, I didn't want to rock the boat and push him too much. I didn't get the feeling he was omitting anything monumental, but there was a dark secret there for sure.

In any case, I had settled in fantastically and was feeling stable and hopeful for the first time in a long time. I really liked Logan and appreciated his kindness so much! I cleaned the house (not that it was the least bit dirty), planted flowers in the yard, started running all of his errands, and actually fixed his leaky faucet! I was particularly proud of that last one! I kindly reminded him that he didn't have to wear the hood all the time, but I knew he felt better with it on, so I continued to allow him to use the hood as a type of security to hide behind. He seemed delicate but with a lurking strength. I figured I could get him to trust me and to break out of his comfort zone after a while.

Logan was thankful he didn't have to go out in public during the last four days, but I didn't think it was healthy to hide away. He told me that most of the year-rounders in the community knew about him and his situation, but that didn't stop them from gawking. They were in no hurry to run up to him and start chatting about the weather either. It was profoundly shameful that modern society still attached such stigma to people who were different - for whatever reason.

The police were well aware of who Logan was, thanks to the 200+ calls they received about a hooded man running around whenever he went out. They were nice enough, though, just tired of the phone calls. Logan mentioned people seemed to stop caring so much about his hood during the pandemic, figuring it was some kind of ultra-precautionary face covering.

According to Logan, teenagers were the worst. He valiantly tried not to blame them, but they could be aggressively mean-spirited and, in some cases, violent. Kids have the potential to be so wicked, but it's usually the parents who are at fault. Children are just curious and want to know things;

it's only after adults teach them to be fearful of differences that it becomes a problem.

Logan managed to teach himself some martial arts by watching online videos after one kid tried to beat the shit out of him. Watching self-defense videos online was seemingly his only exercise, but he had pretty much given up on it. He was pudgy and out of shape but possessed a stubborn endurance when he wanted it.

I liked to do yoga with videos on YouTube, which is where I saw his martial arts viewing history. I strongly urged him to get back into the training - and by urge, I mean I haven't shut up about it. I actually made him promise to start training with me on Monday, to which he begrudgingly agreed. Aside from letting me into his house and life after threatening him with a samurai sword, his willingness to do things outside of his comfort zone led me to believe he had a soft spot for me. He clearly didn't have many friends; it made me very sad to see such a kind soul so lonesome.

Per Logan's request, I have been preparing all our food. I go out of my way to offer healthy yet delicious meals, and for the most part, and as far as I know, they seem to be a big hit!

Logan was quick to point out that in his former life, he only ate healthy out of the necessity of appearance but never took the time to try and enjoy it. He ate at restaurants that were a thousand dollars a plate and never once appreciated what he was eating. I couldn't believe it!

He maintained he couldn't wait to try the food I made because I had awakened his taste buds! I believe the sentiment was genuine, and I was so happy to help him have a better relationship with food. Being an aspiring chef, this meant a lot to me!

Gone now was the vicious cycle of eating garbage food for that temporary high, followed by the crushing regret and realization that he was killing himself with Snickers bars. This dude ate so many Snickers! He had a true obsession with sweets. I was surprised he hadn't put himself into a diabetic coma.

In just four days, my life had changed profoundly. I really enjoyed Logan's company. I didn't feel like I had to entertain him, and he didn't feel like he had to entertain me. We had very complementary personalities, and it made things effortless.

I couldn't help but think Logan might have been crushing on me a little bit - a lady knows, but it was actually very flattering. He was brilliant, talented and extremely nice. He showed me some pictures of himself before his condition, and I was amazed at how handsome he was. Honestly, his current appearance didn't turn me off at all because his personality was so intriguing. Logan said I wouldn't have given him the time of day back when he was attractive because he was such a vapid prick, but I find that hard to believe. I told him it's the person he is now that matters, not the person he was.

Natish called to see how everything was going and to confirm we would still be there for the BBQ the following day. I gave a glowing review of my time here so far but faltered slightly when asked about the BBQ.

Logan was in the other room, trying to be quiet, but I could tell he was listening. It was kind of cute, honestly. I assured Natish that I would be at the BBQ but that I wasn't so certain about Logan. I heard the floor creak as he crept closer to my room, trying to hear what we were talking about.

"Well, I've brought it up a few times, but I'm getting the feeling he's not quite ready to dive into a huge social gathering," I said. "He's said he really likes you and your family, just might have a few issues with large groups of people."

I hated speaking for him like that, but I was getting the feeling that I understood him pretty well. Logan wasn't that dissimilar from me; insecure, angry, and slightly broken. I truly wanted to go, and I believed I could get Logan to go as well.

"Let me call you back," I whispered into the phone and hung up. I began walking out of the room, and I heard Logan quickly tip-toeing into an adjacent room, acting like he was doing something other than listening in.

"Oh, stop it; I know you were listening," I said, chuckling. "Natish just called. Am I going to be able to convince you to go tomorrow?"

Logan's back was to me; I could see his shoulders drop solemnly. He pulled out a pad and pen and wrote, "I REALLY want to go, but I just don't know if I can handle it. I've been away from the human race for quite some time, you know."

"I completely understand, Logan. I do," I said reassuringly. "Buuuuuuut, I think it's really important for you to rejoin society - however awful and shitty it may be. I know it's hard, and I won't press you on it, but if you can muster the courage, I think it would be good for you. Besides, you'll have the hottest date there, so who gives a shit what people think?"

He pondered for a moment and wrote, "I can't guarantee I'll be able to follow through come crunch time, but...I'll try. Thank you for trying to get me to go; you're a really good friend to me. And you're incredibly hot."

"Truer words have never been spoken!" I shouted while laughing. "Alright, alright. Let's talk about what's going to make you feel better about going to this BBQ."

Logan imitated drinking a big bottle of booze, then pointed to his hooded face and made the sign for "erase." I was a quick study when it came to learning sign language, so I understood exactly what he had said.

"Booze, we can do, but it hurts my heart to think you want to erase your face, Logan. I'm starting to think you believe you deserve this condition," I said, emphasizing the word 'condition' with the sign for disease.

He wrote on the pad, "I didn't teach you the sign for disease; have you been studying on your own?"

"Don't change the subject, and yes, I have," I said while signing 'subject' and 'yes.'

Logan nodded, chuckled, and wrote on the pad, "If I'm being honest, I do."

"Why in the hell do you feel like you deserve to be disfigured, Logan?"

He thought long and hard about this and motioned for me to follow him into the living room. I obliged.

Logan grabbed his laptop, took a deep breath, and wrote on the pad, "I really value your friendship and can't tell you how much I appreciate what you've done for me these last few days. It's important you know that before I show you this, I will completely understand if you want to leave."

What could be on his laptop that was so terrible? I continued to look on fretfully as he opened the laptop.

He typed Logan Lepozod into Google's search engine, and sure enough, there at the top was a YouTube video with some kind of art magazine interview.

Logan wrote on his computer, "All those fucking paintings I did, all that work, and this is my legacy." He hit play...

I watched the interview intently and slowly shut the laptop when it was over. I took a deep breath in, exhaled, and looked into Logan's eyes.

He wrote, "What I did to John is my greatest shame. It was me at my ugliest - my worst. I will never forgive myself for acting in such a premeditated, diabolical way. This disease is simply my inner ugliness manifesting itself."

I took a moment to consider things, "I'm not gonna lie, Logan; It's amazingly awful what you did to John - awful in an I-wish-I-could-have-done-that-to-Bryce kind of way, but you aren't that person anymore," I said softly.

"How do you know I'm not that person anymore?" Logan wrote.

"Because you're worried about being that person. Horrible people don't worry about being horrible people; they just are horrible because they don't care. I mean...shit, I'll make sure I never piss you off, but we all do a million different fucked up things for a million different reasons. That doesn't mean we have to put ourselves in prison or consider a disease retribution for being a - granted - uniquely imaginative, long-game asshole. Right?"

Logan

I couldn't believe it. To have someone like Tess tell me I wasn't a monster and accept the terrible thing I did with such grace and ease was like having a battleship removed from my chest.

"What I did was unforgivable, Tess."

"Why don't you ask John if what you did was unforgivable and go from there?"

The thought pierced my heart like an arrow. I had never even considered trying to track John down and talk it out.

"You just assumed your condition was some kind of cosmic sentence imposed upon you by the universe for being a giant, rotten dick. If that's prison worthy, I'll be in the cell next to you. I think this face of yours is the best thing that ever happened to you. It made your inner ugliness...beautiful. Beau-laid..." she said with a chuckle and smile to herself.

I was floored. A lifetime of pain, regret, and sadness was put into perspective within five minutes by a wayward angel who was bamboozled by a wannabe pimp named Bryce. With so many thoughts swimming through my head, one struck me: beau-laid.

I wrote, "Beau-laid?"

She smiled deeper, "It's something my mother used to say to me. It's French like she was. It means...beautiful because of our flaws. It's how she always described my father. She would always say, 'I'm in love with him because his flaws make him real, not because he's perfect. He's beau-laid.' God, that was a lifetime ago," Tess reflected with tears threatening her eyes.

This woman had layers. Many, many wonderful and compelling layers. I couldn't wait to spend whatever time she afforded me discovering as many of those layers as I could.

"I love the idea of my flaws being beautiful, but I'm as ugly on the inside as I am on the outside," I wrote on the last line of the last sheet on my pad.

Tess read this and shook her head. "I'm having a really hard time believing you're ugly on the inside, Logan. You think you're ugly on the outside, but you're absolutely wrong, which means you're likely wrong about being ugly on the inside. I don't see people in such stark black and whites." She thought for a moment, "That's what made me so vulnerable to someone like Bryce. He immediately pegged me for a mark because of all my blah, blah, blahing about shit like that. I gave him the blueprint to manipulate me. I'm such a damn fool."

I spoke for the first time in roughly five years, "Don't...EVER...call yourself...foolish for...being...so...lovely." I couldn't believe my own ears when I heard the words come out of my mouth. While muffled, dusty and gravely, the words meant more to me than anything I had ever said.

Tess looked into my eyes, cocked her head in that quizzical way, wiped her tears away and stood up. She walked over to me, thoughtfully pulled off my hood, leaned down, and lightly kissed me where my lips used to be. "This is how I know you aren't a horrible person," she said. "In fact, I think we're very much alike."

Chapter Five

Does it hurt?

Logan

I woke up the next morning a completely different person. I didn't even recognize myself in the mirror when I reported for my daily defamation. It didn't seem right anymore. Things had changed. My face was still there, but the monster was gone. I cried.

I floated through the house without my hood like a spirit, untethered and weightless. I seriously felt like I might drift away into the atmosphere. Every moment from this point forward was effortless.

I decided three things during the course of the night: one, I would find John and face the music. No longer would I hide like a coward in a prison of my own design because I was unable to accept what I had done. Whether he forgave me or not, I owed it to him to simply apologize.

Second, I was going to this goddamned BBQ if it killed me. After all, it was a BBQ, not the fucking Spanish Inquisition, and I wanted to show Natish and her family how much I liked them.

I also wanted to prove to Tess I was capable of bravery and growth. These would be the first steps toward my rejoining the world.

Finally, I was totally in love with Tess. There was no denying it. There was no compartmentalizing it, and there was no avoiding it. I also realized there was no way to pursue it. I didn't want to jeopardize our friendship or burden her with the awkwardness of it all anyway.

I decided I would show my love by being a good friend and supporting her. The last thing she needed was my damaged affection.

Tess

I came into the kitchen as Logan was making breakfast and pressing the coffee. The morning sun filtered in through the window from behind, giving the kitchen a heavenly glow. There at the center was Logan. No one had ever cooked for me before Logan, and it pulled on my heartstrings. I also entertained the idea that he was making breakfast so he could have bacon, eggs, and biscuits.

"That better be an eggwhite omelet with spinach I smell!" I jokingly demanded.

"Of course," Logan said with some effort. He decided to sign the rest, "This diet is amazing! The food is delicious, and I've already lost a few pounds!"

I signed back clumsily, "Good! Coffee now!"

He laughed and handed me a cup with almond milk- no sugar in it, just the way I liked it. "Thank you, Logan," I said sweetly. "I'm so pleased you like the diet!"

I knew he didn't like the diet one bit. While he seemed to really enjoy the food, the portions were anorexic, and I could tell he was constantly starving. Fortunately, he had amazing willpower; I only caught him cheating once.

I know he hasn't cheated since because I read him the riot act. Now he's opted for trying to fudge the rules a bit by doing things like making breakfast with bacon. I didn't mind, though; it was sweet.

I think Logan began to realize just how much he had been eating his depression over the last five years. Fortunately, it didn't seem that difficult for him to fall back into healthy eating habits. The real struggle came when I tried to cut him down to one scotch a night! He definitely didn't strike me as having a drinking problem, and he never said anything when I discreetly puffed a joint here and there, so I let it slide.

What really struck me this morning was the absence of Logan's hood!

"No hood! I likey, I likey!!" I said sincerely.

Logan framed his face with his hands and curtsied.

Giggling, I asked if he wanted to do some yoga before "Maaaaaybe" going to the BBQ.

He surprised me by confidently signing, "I would love to do some yoga!" Then he spoke with embellished ability, "and...I would...LOVE to go to...the...BBQ!"

"Squeeeeeeeeeeee," I squealed while clapping my hands together! "I'm so glad to hear that! Really! Still, if you feel like you need to wait, there's no pressure!"

Logan opted to write on his pad since I still didn't know a lot of the words he signed, and he was still getting used to trying to talk, "It would be my absolute honor and privilege to escort you to the BBQ, my lady."

"Ohhhh, 'my lady,' I like that!"

He wrote, "Big question, hood on or off?"

I was so overcome, I couldn't resist holding his face in my hands, "Off," I whispered.

He sighed deeply but nodded. "Okay."

"Yay! I'm so excited! I haven't looked forward to anything in forever," I announced between sips of coffee. I could read the apprehension in his eyes, "Don't worry, I'll be right there with you! If it's a failure, it will be a FANTASTIC failure!"

Logan lightly touched my elbow, "Thank you, Tess."

"You're on Team Tess now; I got you!" I promised, pouring some more coffee. "Alright, let's eat and do some yoga!"

"Yay," Logan grumbled unceremoniously.

Logan

Needless to say, my body did not want to do yoga, but I wanted to do yoga with Tess, so I struggled through it.

"That's the spirit!" Tess said triumphantly as I tried to do a particularly difficult pose.

Within a few seconds, I crumpled to the floor. This shit was hard!

"Awww, c'mon, I was just starting to get impressed!"

I laughed and waved my hands to say, "No more!"

"I know what you need!" She grabbed up the remote and scrolled through the history until she came across a self-defense video. "Here we go! This may be more up your alley right now."

I slouched and looked at her defeatedly. "Please, God, no more," I signed with my exhausted hands.

"Shuddup, this is happening," she said matter-of-factly.

Tess located a fun looking self-defense video titled: 'Back Alley Blitzkrieg' and queued it up. "Alright, big guy, on your feet! This one looks particularly violent; let's do it!"

I struggled to my feet and positioned myself. I vaguely remembered watching this one before, but we watched it a couple of times to get the moves down. She asked if I was ready, and I reluctantly shook my head.

"Okay, attack me, Logan!"

I moved in slowly with my hands outstretched, like the assailant pictured in the video, and put my hands delicately on her shoulders. Tess reacted like a sprung trap! She clapped her hands together like she was praying, rammed them up between my arms, and forcibly extended them apart! Without warning, she expertly grabbed the fingers on my right hand with her left hand, twisted them palm up towards the sky, and forced me down to my right knee!

Then she delivered the coup de gras with a high-arching knife-hand straight to my throat! Fortunately for me, she didn't follow through with the strike, but if she had, I would have been done for. She released me, so I slowly got to my feet.

Holy shit, Tess was a badass! “Wasn’t expecting that,” I managed to say!

“Haha, well, I used to take Krav Maga, so...” Tess blew on her nails and confidently polished them on her tank top.

I started signing with my right hand, feigned extreme pain, and started signing with my left while speaking the words, “You’re a badass!”

“I wouldn’t go that far,” she said, scoffing, ” but it’s how I managed to get away from...Bryce,” his name darkening the mood.

Using both hands to sign along with my speech, “Please tell me you got a good shot in!”

“I’m pretty sure I broke his finger, and I managed to pull a huge chunk of his hair out,” Tess spoke through a growing smile.

“Atta girl,” I said.

“He was crying when I ran off. Damn, I should have stomped him one more time right in the balls!” She said, emphasizing “balls” energetically with sign language.

We both burst out laughing.

“Okay, okay, my turn,” I signed while also trying to say it.

“Alright, big boy, show me what you got!”

Tess moved in with speed and agility, grabbed me by my shirt, and started shaking me like a redheaded stepchild!

I reacted quickly and admirably managed to break her hold and grab her fingers! However, when I went for my coup de gras, she grabbed my wrist and rolled me to the floor! In a flash, she was on top of me with her hand at my throat!

“You’re dead!” She bellowed and started tickling me relentlessly!

I, being extremely ticklish, began bucking like a bronco and desperately tried to get away! She got off me and helped me up, "Now I know your Kryptonite, Logan - tickling!"

I gasped and caught my breath, "You suck!"

"Careful with that mouth; I'll tickle your ass to death!"

"It wouldn't surprise me if you did," I signed. "You're diabolical," I added in broken speech.

"I guess I am kind of a badass!"

"And then some," I said.

"Hi-ya!" Tess shouted, chopping the air!

"Alright, Logan. Are you ready for this?" Tess inquired while looking me full on in the eyes.

"I am," I said while nodding my hoodless head.

"Okay then!" She threw open my front door, held out her arm, and I took it. "Sir..."

I escorted her out the door, off the porch, and into the complete unknown.

I felt the warm breeze, carrying the scent of honeysuckle, blowing gently over my face, and it awakened me in such a compelling way. I can't believe I never took the time to appreciate it before! The things you take for granted are often never realized. If not for my affliction, I would have just carried on through life, asleep to all its beautiful wonder.

Having Tess with me erased the fear and insecurity of being seen and allowed me to fully appreciate the world around me. It occurred to me that I had lived my entire life up to this point, both handsome and ugly, terrified of people's judgment.

Because of my enfeebling insecurities, I had been missing so much. For so long. I thought stature, looks, money, and things were what made life worth living, but after only a minute outside with Tess, on a regular day, my eyes were opened to it all.

I needed someone like Tess to show me that the little things were what mattered, and that happiness truly takes shape when shared with someone close to your heart.

I would have wasted my entire life, having missed all these wonderful feelings, had I not met Tess.

The trees, birds, sun, flowers - all had been wasted on me but now hit my senses through a different lens of perception. I had painted so many beautiful things but was myself blind to it all until now. I was close to being overwhelmed by the experience of my heart soaring like never before!

Then my neighbor, who had been walking her dog on the same side of the street as us, suddenly noticed me and froze dead in her tracks. She knew she was caught and uncomfortably fumbled with her phone in order to occupy her eyes as we passed by. Quick as a shot, my soaring heart tried to nosedive, but there was Tess...

"Just relax, Logan. People are going to be caught off guard by you," she whispered into my ear as we walked by. I didn't realize it, but I was holding her hand so tight that my knuckles were white.

"People are going to gawk at you. People are going to be rude to you. People are going to say and do terrible things to you, all because you are different. But the reality is, they would be doing those things anyway, regardless of how you look or who you are. That's just people. Worrying about it robs you of the world's beauty."

Tess was right, of course, and suddenly I didn't care what my neighbor thought; or anyone else for that matter! I mean, who gives a fuck!? I don't care that my neighbor has more botox in her head than sense, so why do I care what she thinks about me!? Another colossal weight was leaving me!

Tess continued, "I mean, while you were all focused on her being focused on you, you may have missed something really important...or hilarious."

I looked at Tess and cocked my head the way she always did. Tess snickered and pointed nonchalantly after my neighbor, who was hurrying away from the situation. I followed her finger with my eyes, and there, trailing my neighbor, was about two feet of toilet paper hanging out of the waistband of her culottes. As if that wasn't enough, there was also a slight brown streak down the middle of the paper ribbon that looked to be rubbing off on her pants. I don't know about you, but I'd rather be disfigured in public than shit-covered in public.

"Now see, the old Logan would have missed that entirely! But the new Logan doesn't flinch, doesn't turn away, and doesn't care about what people think. That Logan gets to see the toilet paper hanging out of a wannabe Kardashian's butt. Boom."

"I think...I...love you," I blurted out! Jesus Christ, I hope that was too garbled to understand!

"How could you not?" Tess said sweetly without missing a beat.

As we got closer to Natish's house, more and more people were out in the streets headed that way. There were a few double takes, but for the most part, no one seemed to care about my face! Funny how I used to demand the spotlight, and now I just wanted to be overlooked. I was still riding the high of Tess's poignant insight, though, so I just powered through.

I could feel Tess looking for signs of apprehension, but I was honestly okay. I felt amazing! We joked the last two blocks before arriving at Natish's house, and I was ready to rejoin the world.

There were tons of people. There were people in the street, there were people in the courtyard, there were people in the house, there were people everywhere! A mere week ago, I would have collapsed before even stepping foot out of my front door, but I felt invincible with Tess at my side.

We searched for Natish and finally found her in the kitchen, with whom we could only assume were her two sisters and mother, based on the family resemblance and their shenanigans with one another. They were slaving away over a massive oven while arguing, laughing, shouting, whispering, and pinching each other!

Natish caught sight of us and threw her hands up in excitement! "There they are! Get on in here, and grab something to drink! We got ever'thing here from diddled-eyed-Joe, to damned if I know!" Natish's mom smacked her butt and shook her finger at her as if to say, "Watch that mouth!"

"What!?" Natish huffed!

"You know I don't tolerate no cussing 'round here!" Her mother scolded.

As I poured myself a tumbler of single-malt, Tess grabbed a seltzer water, and Natish introduced us to her mother and sisters. "This is my momma, Nanny, and these are my two sisters, Gina and Roshanda. Nanny, Gina, and Roshanda, this here is my new bestie, Tess! And this, ladies, is my favorite artist of all time, and world-renowned painter, Logan Lepozod! Show them some love!"

I felt like I was being introduced on The Late Show!

Without hesitation, all three women scooped us up in a loving group hug and shook us like family! "I hope you're hungry," Nanny announced, "Y'all gonna bust at the seams when we're done wit'cha!" Nanny, standing only about five-foot-tall, turned and pulled two huge, round cast-iron pans out of the oven with cornbread that smelled the way I imagined Heaven should smell!

I figured the two cast-iron pans weighed significantly more than Nanny, but she handled them with skill and grace.

Suddenly, Gina handed Tess an apron, and Roshanda handed her an oven mitt, "Since you're family now," Gina stated, "grab that cornbread and follow me out back! And be careful; that's honest-to-God, southern, skillet-style cornbread! Nanny's recipe!"

"I wouldn't dream of dropping this!" Tess promised.

I watched nervously as Gina escorted Tess out of the kitchen, leaving me without my social safety net, and I instantly felt a wave of intense insecurity trying to wash over me like the dead sea.

Before I even had a chance to feel the stones in my stomach turn over, Roshanda slapped an apron and an oven mitt against my belly, "You ain't gettin' out of helping! Now, grab that other pan of cornbread, those beans, and let's feed the masses!" She flashed a very warm smile, "Follow me!"

Once we had all the food out, and it was A LOT of food, we sat down and took a rest to let others get their plates. There was such a wonderful mixture of people present, and they all seemed concerned with a million different things, none of them my face.

I suppose it's presumptuous and self-centered of me to think everyone would be so interested in my face, but old habits die hard. Even the kids and teens were too preoccupied with the festivities to give me more than a passing glance. It was wonderful!

Apparently, I love BBQ. Tess said this could be my cheat day, but I could see her watching me. I made sure to reign my stomach in, but it wasn't easy. The ribs, cornbread, pulled pork, beef tips, potato salad, slaw, et cetera, et cetera were absolutely amazing! I couldn't believe I had lived my entire life up to this point without having real southern style BBQ.

Nanny kept trying to push more food on me, but I had to call it quits. I had managed to lose three pounds in five days, and I wasn't about to forfeit the momentum. Tess, thankfully, ran interference; it seemed they were even more obsessed with cramming food down her throat! She was such a tiny thing; they were concerned she wasn't eating enough at my house.

Tess spent an hour prying the recipes and secrets from Nanny's mental archive, promising never to divulge them to anyone else. I was hoping to benefit from some of those recipes since my diet was so stringent. That said, Tess knew a hundred different, delicious ways to prepare skinless chicken and kale, so it wasn't all bad.

"Does it hurt?" I looked down from my chair to see Natish's daughter, Nina, shyly standing there by my side.

"Sometimes," I managed. "Mostly, it's...just hard...to talk."

"Oh," she said softly. "Wanna play Pokemon Go?"

"I would...love to."

"Yay!" She suddenly proclaimed and grabbed my hand to lead me away.

Tess

Natish and I both looked over with matching smiles as Nina dragged Logan away to hunt Pokemon. "Well, now if that ain't the cutest thing ever," Natish admitted.

"Nina is such a sweet girl," I said, beaming. "Did you ask her to go play with Logan?"

"Me? Hell no, that child does whatever she wants to!" Natish gave a throaty laugh. "She is an excellent judge of character too, just like her Momma," she said, followed by a long sip of wine!

"Well, her mother is an excellent teacher!"

"Better than she is a student," Natish said dreamily before snapping around to reality. "So, how's everything going at

Casa Logan? You guys seem like you're getting on pretty well."

"We are!" I said enthusiastically. "He's really opening up, but I worry about him," I confided, my brow wrinkling. "He sincerely thinks he doesn't deserve to be happy. It hurts me to see him that way. Logan is such a kind and special person; I wish he could see that."

"Well, maybe that's why the two of you met the way you did," Natish said in a serious tone. "You teach him to see his worth and be happy; maybe he'll teach you the same. Be good for both of you."

Natish raised her head a bit and smelled the air. "I tell you, it just doesn't get any better than this. Family and friends on a summer afternoon; bellies full; warm breeze. Now, this is what I call a Saturday!"

"Natish?"

"Yes, love?"

"You say you know a lot about Logan...Did you ever see that interview he did for "The Global Arts?"

"Oh honey, I did indeed," Natish said in a pointed voice. "That boy was hardcore. Honestly, it's the reason I bought my first painting of his. After seeing the interview, I looked up his art online and fell in love with it. Once I saw the painting, I forgot all about that cold-ass shit he pulled. How'd *you* come across it?"

"He showed me. It was like watching a completely different person," I said in a hushed voice.

"Yeah, but he was hot as hell, wasn't he!?"

"Oh my God, so hot!" I said too loud while laughing.

"Well, he may have been capable of that kind of deviltry in the past, but it's definitely not the vibe I'm reading now. Seems to me he's found his heart." Natish thought about it for a second, then added, "He sweet on you?"

"Oh, I don't think so, at least not in that way," I said, blushing. "He's been nothing but kind and gentlemanly since I met him."

"Don't forget, he may be a changed man, but he's all about that long-game. I'd be really careful about leading him on," Natish warned.

"Oh, absolutely! I would never lead him on if I wasn't interested," I blurted out, blushing even more.

"Mmm hmmm. You, ah...sweet on *him*?" Natish asked carefully.

I looked at Natish, then looked away. I thought about it for a long moment before answering, "Honestly...maaaaaybe just a little," I confessed, holding up my first finger a half an inch above my thumb. "Is that weird?"

"Hell no," Natish said definitively. "The heart wants what it wants, girl. And if we're being perfectly honest, I'd be a little sweet on him too. He's so...complex. Mysterious. Not to mention kind and interesting. I certainly don't see anything wrong with it," Natish said, taking a long pull off her wine. "There ain't no shame in the game, girl. I say go for it! That said, you better be careful with people who are clearly vulnerable in a profound way, and I'm talking about both of you."

"I know, I know," I reassured Natish. "I don't even know how I would approach it. But I can tell you this, Logan seems to be everything I ever wanted in a man. Naturally, when I pictured my dream guy, he was this dashing and handsome commercial cutout, but that really doesn't matter to me. I look at his face, and all I see is a sweet, talented, and beautiful man."

Natish chimed in, "Honestly, I still find him to be...unconventionally attractive. His face is bold, cut, striking, interesting - I know how that sounds, but really. It's like all his handsome features have been magnified and chiseled. Now, if he lost a few L B's, cut up a bit, and got healthy, I could hit that. Shit, I could almost climb him based on his paintings alone; dude is plugged in." Natish slapped her hip and began laughing.

"What do you think I should do, Natish?"

"I think you should let your heart lead you. I know it sounds cliche, but I saw a spark between you two right away, and that's absolutely worth exploring. Like I said, I not only liked you and Logan both right away, but I liked the dynamic between you. There's something there, and I support you one hundred percent in whatever you decide to do."

We both looked over at Logan playing with Nina and smiled deeply.

"Well, he's good with kids," I said more to myself than Natish. Coming back to Earth, "I'll just wait and see how things develop organically."

"Absolutely. Don't force anything and just see what's what!" A silence hung in the air for a moment before Natish asked, "Is he still painting?"

I was saddened a bit by this, "I haven't seen him paint, or even seen a studio for that matter. I saw a bunch of supplies in the basement, but they had about five years' worth of dust on them. I was planning on asking him about it next week. I think it would be good for him to start painting again."

"Absolutely! And, uh, if it's not too much trouble, I need some new material for my collection - if you know what I mean," Natish explained jovially. "Man, I wish he'd get back into it. I would represent the shit out of him."

"Represent?" I asked.

"Yeah! I mean, I typically represent musicians and actors, but I don't see any reason I couldn't be his agent. In any case, it's my agency, so I can do whatever the hell I want to. I could easily get his career back on track!"

"He already has an incredible body of work; it wouldn't take that much to get him going again. I'd have to do some research into the fine arts, but I wager it's not so dissimilar from what I'm doing now. I would absolutely relish the opportunity to represent my favorite painter! Hell, if I can get Furious raking in cash off his poetry, I can blow Logan back up! It's kind of my thing," Natish said proudly.

"Wow! That would be amazing! I'll have a talk with him about picking up the brush again and feel him out. That's so thoughtful, Natish, thank you!"

"Of course, Tess. I like the two of you, and that does NOT happen often," she said, laughing her throaty laugh. "I'm pulling for ya both!"

We shared another smile and brightened each other's disposition.

Logan

Nina ran off to capture more Pokemon as I tumbled exhaustively into a patio chair. I looked back just in time to see Tess and Natish's beautiful smiles. They were both so lovely. Their presence in my life was providential. Looking at them made me want to paint them exactly as I saw them. Even though I hadn't picked up a brush in roughly five years, I could feel my mind taking a snapshot of the scene for later reference, which used to be my process. I hadn't felt like painting since my fleeting series did so poorly many years ago. I just didn't feel inspired like I did right now. I don't think I ever felt as inspired as I did right at that moment.

Tess caught me looking and sweetly waved. When anyone caught my eye, I always looked away, but this time I was mesmerized. I waved back slowly with my heart more than my hand.

Her smile widened...then died.

It was like a knife piercing my soul until I realized Tess wasn't looking at me anymore but rather past me. I followed her gaze, which led my eyes to an ostentatiously dressed, flashy but handsome man with a crew cut, and a broken finger.

It hit me all at once - this was Bryce.

A rage ignited within me, the likes of which I hadn't known possible! I stood and slowly turned to fully face him with the sole intention of ripping his throat out. Suddenly, there was a soft hand on my shoulder.

Tess

"It's okay, Logan. No need to worry about him," I reassured Logan.

Natish was right behind me, "What's up, you two?! This guy a problem?"

Logan was too flustered to eke out a response, but I quietly told Natish what the situation was, "That's Bryce."

"Ohhhhhhhh *HEEEEEELL* no. Not at my party, motherfucker!"

Before Natish could roll over there and eviscerate him, I quieted her. "It's okay; I got my licks in on him. Having said that, I fully support making someone like that leave."

"It's gonna be more than that; somebody about to get they ass pulled through their fuckin' mouth!" Natish growled, shedding her polished exterior. "I will rain sulfur down on his fool head."

Before Natish could salt the Earth under his feet, Bryce recognized me and sauntered over. "Hey there, Tess! Fancy seeing you here. Been a minute, bitch. I believe I owe you one," he said, raising his splinted fingers.

"If it's a rematch you're looking for, you better grow some balls first," I said, gently holding Natish back.

Bryce suddenly looked at Logan and burst out laughing. "Well, I can see you traded up after I left you! Holy shit, dude, you look like a meatball's asshole!"

Logan took a definitive step forward, but I held him back with my other arm.

"Don't tell me you're gettin' froggy, fuck face!" Bryce said to Logan, his entourage taking notice of the raised voices.

They circled around us as Bryce continued with his childish insults. “You might wanna reconsider that, Mr. Meatball. Me and my boys here will fuck you up back to handsome.”

Natish guffawed, “You fuckin’ twerpy-ass, candy-colored douche bag. The only thing you and these fuckin’ sugar-free thugs are gonna fuck up is that walkway as y’all walkin’ ya asses the fuck outta here!”

When Natish’s fuse was lit, she lost all of her polish and sprouted horns! Bryce laughed at her, but I cut him off with a smack to his lips. It happened so fast that I didn’t even realize I had done it!

Bryce tried to get in my face, but Logan had finally had enough. He stepped in between us and stood his ground.

“Hey, look, Meatball’s got balls!” Bryce said as he started poking Logan in the chest with his good fingers.

Without warning, Logan snatched up Bryce’s fingers, the exact same way we had practiced not six hours earlier and twisted his hand towards the sky with enough force to snap at least two of them!

Bryce howled in pain as Logan kicked his knee out from under him and sent him to the ground. Logan had him on his knees crying out when a fist suddenly struck the side of his head!

Logan was dazed but still managed to jump on Bryce and pound his face into pudding! Suddenly, a massive meat hook dragged Logan off of him and hoisted him into the air like a ragdoll. Logan dangled there for a moment before the linebacker who had him was tackled to the ground!

I was shocked to see it was Furious who blindsided the mountain of a man who had manhandled Logan. Within seconds, Furious had him on the ground and was now dolling out a beat-down!

Bryce's entourage quickly moved in, but Furious's multitude of friends, many of whom were much bigger than Bryce's biggest, were right there to have his back!

Furious jumped off the big fella whose nose fountained blood and readied himself for any comers. "ALRIGHT! That's it for you youngsters!" Furious shouted as he reached down and grabbed Bryce by his ear like an irate parent might grab their insubordinate child. He gave Bryce's ear a hard twist and began dragging him towards the exit.

While pulling him asshole over elbow, Furious scolded him, "This is why we can't have nice things! Motherfucker, you're lucky I'm not breaking my foot off in your ass for fucking up my baby's BBQ!"

"I'm sorry, I'm sorry," Bryce pleaded, but Furious wasn't having it. Once they were at the gate, Furious flung it open, grabbed Bryce by the collar of his shirt and the waistband of his pants, and heaved him out into the yard like a bouncer! "Don't come back now, ya hear!"

Furious turned an angry eye to Bryce's people and hooked his thumb, "Get the fuck outta here."

Bryce's booty crew looked around and weighed the odds. Apparently, they didn't like them much because they reluctantly followed Furious's thumb out the gate.

Bryce jumped to his feet when he was surrounded by his protectors again, "Yeah, fuck ALL Y'ALL! This is some bullshit!" Then he caught my eye, "This ain't over, meatball! You and that stupid cunt are dead! Imma fuck all you bitches up!!"

"You better get the fuck offa my lawn," Furious proclaimed!

Bryce and his boys slowly turned and walked away.

Furious slammed the gate closed and turned back around to face everyone who was still frozen silently in place.

Beating his chest like King Kong, he hollered out, "I'm FUUUUURIOUS!" Everyone burst out laughing and went back to partying.

Furious hurried over to us and fretted over Natish. "Are you okay, baby!"

"I'm fine, my love. Thank you for taking out the trash."

"Damn right. Tess, you and Logan, okay!?"

We both nodded as Logan tried to get to his feet.

"Logan, you are FIERCE, brother!" Furious said as he helped him up.

Laughing, Logan wiped a bit of blood from his mouth, "Not so much."

"As long as you can still paint and kick-ass, we good!"

Logan tested his hand and gave the thumbs up.

I immediately grabbed Logan in a bear hug and kissed him right on the small area of his exposed lips! "Thank you, Logan!"

He hugged me back tightly, "It's no trouble!"

"Is everyone else okay," I asked, genuinely concerned.

Natish and Furious looked intently at us as we looked intently at them. Once we were certain everyone was okay, Natish spoke, "Who needs a damn drink?"

We all raised our hands in unison!

"Fuckin' A," Furious said in an exasperated tone.

Logan

As the party began to wind down around ten, I helped Natish and her sisters clean up. Her family was amazing. Her daughter, Nina, had become my new best friend. As I put chairs and tables away, she educated me about all the different Pokemon and their abilities. Really quite interesting, if I'm being honest.

Gina had to come and drag Nina away for bed, but Nina made me promise I would play Pokemon with her again. I promised I would and even made plans to download the app on my phone.

Tess came up from behind and wrapped her arms softly around me. "My hero," she whispered into my ear. "Still, you know I could have kicked his ass again, right?"

I squeezed her arms and turned around within them so we were face-to-face. I was too exhausted from speaking so much in one day, so I just nodded.

After a moment, she released me, and I signed to her with my hands, "I wanted a piece too, don't hog all the badass!"

"You want to hog a piece of my ass?" Tess said, raising her eyebrows. She was still learning.

I snickered loudly and took out my pad and pen. "I wanted a piece too, don't hog all the badass!"

"Ohhhhhh, okay! Yeah, that makes more sense!" Tess said, laughing. "Still, I think we should take his threat seriously. He may be a wormy piece of shit, but he's connected. We should tell Natish and Furious to keep their eyes open."

I nodded and wrote, “Absolutely! Although I feel very sorry for them if they come back to this house looking for trouble.”

“Agreed,” Tess said in a worried tone. “Where are Natish and Furious? I wanted to thank them for such a wonderful time...and apologize for my situation causing drama.”

“Are you kidding me?” I wrote. “That piece of shit would have been here regardless; thanks to you, they knew to throw them out!”

“Yeah, I guess so. Let’s go find them before I fall asleep!”

Chapter Six

Payne's Gray

Logan

This morning, two months later, I felt amazing! I felt like I had finally cracked the shell of my cocoon and was ready to fully emerge! The sun was shining, the leaves were exploding with color, it was still warm, and I felt great!

I had been out of the house without my hood many times now, and it seemed like the locals were getting used to seeing me around. Even my neighbor with the toilet paper ribbon waved cordially to me now. Tess was right; after you dispel the mystery of it all, people move on to other shit to be tight-assed about.

Tess took me to a great restaurant a few weeks ago, and we had a wonderful time! There were a few stares, but it really didn't bother me much anymore. I imagine the experience would be different without Tess there to support me, but I'll take what I can get.

Thanks to Tess, I had lost 20 plus pounds over the last two months and started to see my old muscle tone popping back out! I had forgotten what it was like to have a well-defined body. I still had a fair share of work to do, but I was pleased with my progress. Tess and I were doing martial arts training every morning for several hours, and both of us have gotten pretty damn good!

I also scheduled surgery to have some of the more invasive lipomas removed from my face and mouth because they were starting to give me trouble in the breathing department. I continued to struggle a little with talking, but I was getting considerably better with practice and effort.

I still tried to sign when I talked, though, because it helped Tess with learning her sign language, and it was good for me to keep practicing.

My doctor said I was doing great and that the growths had slowed substantially. Hopefully, after I get the majority of them removed, they won't come back in force for a while.

Tess and I had grown very close in the time she was here. We understood one another and were best friends. I couldn't imagine my life without her, which frightened me beyond belief.

There was a very real possibility that once she was stable, had some savings, and was in a better head-space that she would leave. This thought kept me up at night, but I soldiered on, thankful for any time I was able to spend with her. Even if she did leave, I think she would stay local; Natish and I had become like family to her.

Additionally, I was picking up on a strong attraction between us, but I just couldn't let myself believe it. The crushing disappointment would be too much, and there was a strong possibility I was reading into something that wasn't there.

I studied the blank canvas for what seemed like forever. It was the first time I had begun a painting in over five years. I couldn't believe I had lain dormant for so long. Tess, Natish, and even Furious had been politely pestering me over the past two months to start painting again. Natish even graciously offered to represent me, but I knew I wasn't quite there yet.

Tess could barely hide her excitement as she helped me pull all my art supplies from the basement. My oil paint and mediums had long since dried up, which was disappointing but not surprising. I pulled out my cell phone to order some more when Tess reached out and took hold of my hand.

I looked up to see her standing there, a box at her feet. "I took the liberty of ordering you some paint and supplies about a month ago. I saw all the materials in the basement and just ordered what I saw. I hope I got you the right stuff." She followed the kind sentiment with a glowing smile. God, she was beautiful.

I leaned over and looked inside the box. Sure enough, it was everything I needed. My eyes became dewy with emotion, but I shook it off and nodded, "It's perfect...Thank you, Tess."

I set up my old easel in the living room so I could paint while she watched TV. Tess put on one of her horror movies and pretended to watch it instead of my progress.

I trepidatiously, fearfully, and excitedly raised my brush, almost like a weapon in the hands of a man preparing for war.

Payne's gray, somewhere between black and blue, was ALWAYS my first and favorite color. It represented all of my shadows and was the bedrock foundation for all my paintings. It was like hugging an old friend.

As soon as my brush touched the canvas for the first time after so long, it was like being awoken by lightning. An explosive electrical connection was made between the tip of my brush and the surface of the canvas.

All the dust that had settled upon my life was suddenly blown from my form, and the chains of my past were broken! I felt electrically charged, like I had been on life support, then shocked back to life!

The paintbrush seemed in control of my hand and, without my prompting, began feverishly traveling across its surface, seemingly on its own!

Suddenly, the memory of Tess and Natish sitting and smiling at the BBQ began to take shape. Their forms burst off the canvas, and all the colors, smells, tastes, and feelings of that magical day materialized in my mind!

I even put Furious, Jamal, Nina, Gina, Roshanda, and Nanny in the background. I had seen so much of them over the last two months that their faces appeared to me effortlessly.

I had Furious flexing his warrior muscles; I painted Nanny placing the cornbread on the table, with Gina and Roshanda helping. I put Nina in the foreground, running with her cell phone hunting Pokemon; Natish was comfortably and confidently smiling from her patio chair. And Tess, sweet Tess, was the center of it all. Glowing, she was the light source of the entire painting. All of the shadows and highlights within the painting relied on her for their placement.

Tess

I quietly snuck up behind Logan and breathlessly watched him paint, my hand over my mouth in amazement. He had been standing there painting for six straight hours without a break!

"I am in awe of this painting, Logan!" I whispered. "I sincerely can't believe how beautiful it is! You've captured everyone's likeness and spirit so well!"

He acted as though he were waking from a deep sleep, "I...I'm so pleased you like it!"

"Like is not the word I would use to describe how I feel about this painting," I said, gasping. "I am so honored to be a part of it! There is something missing though..." I started ponderously.

Logan faltered, "What?" He genuinely wanted to know.

"You," I said sweetly. "You deserve to be in this painting more than anyone!"

He sheepishly used sign language instead of talking, which was what he would sometimes do in awkward situations, "I painted this from my perspective, so I didn't include myself."

I scolded him verbally while signing, "Yeah, yeah, yeah, I know what you're up to. I'm not going to be too hard on you, though, because you've done so well about coming out from under the hood. That said, you were the best part of that day for me, and without you, it's missing the magic."

He narrowed his eyes, but I never wavered. He took a deep breath, let it out, and looked at the canvas. "I suppose...I can fit myself in behind you, next to Nina...hunting Pokemon..."

"I think that would be wonderful," I offered, changing back to a gentler tone.

"I appreciate you always pushing me to...evolve," he said in a hushed voice. "I guess once I lost my looks and friends, I just gave up on everything. I was pretty...shallow."

I took his hands in mine and looked him in the eyes, "You are the most beautiful man I have ever known." I suddenly kissed him lovingly on his partially obscured mouth! I was so overcome in the moment that I couldn't help myself. Logan froze in place and then actually pulled away.

"I'm...I'm sorry, Logan. I didn't mean to be presumptuous," The words left my mouth as I held his hands and bowed my head in embarrassment.

"No, no! I Just... wasn't expecting that is all," he blurted out, bringing my hands up to his heart and pressing them there. "Why would you be...the presumptuous one?"

"Well," I said, blushing, "I've been having...*feelings*...and I...just didn't want to...assume that you...you know...you felt the same way..." I managed, the words trailing off gracelessly.

Logan

My heart literally exploded within my chest! Tess could feel it in her hands and pulled her eyes back up to meet mine. I felt like my entire life was building to this moment!

"I've...had...feelings for you...since the day I met you," I revealed sheepishly with muffled words. I felt so exposed and vulnerable but exhilarated all at the same time!

These were not feelings I was used to. I continued to speak, feeling compelled to personally say what my heart demanded, "You are such...a uniquely beautiful-breathtaking presence. I've...never...EVER felt such a strong pull to someone...in my entire life."

Seemingly under the control of a force I did not recognize, I suddenly kissed Tess again! I couldn't believe I did it! I sincerely thought I would never kiss a beautiful woman again, much less feel actual love blooming, but here I was! My entire body was electrified and magnetized. It was surreal, foreign, terrifying, exciting, amazing - overwhelming! The act of painting again after so long, coupled with the first sparks of a flourishing true love, had left my head swimming.

I wanted to freeze this moment for eternity and never leave. The tsunami of emotions that crashed upon my weak and weary heart threatened to literally knock me out! It was a sensation I had never experienced in my 46 years. It's hard to explain, but when I passionately kissed Tess, I had what I can only describe as a legitimate, full body, mental and spiritual...*climax*! It's not like I had an orgasm in the traditional sense, but my entire body and spirit came together, comprised of gunpowder, and she had thrown a match!

Tess

As a woman, I've felt many things during a burgeoning relationship, but *this*, this was something absolutely intoxicating! I felt drugged! I felt transported from reality.

When Logan kissed me, I knew it was right. My heart sang, my spirit shot into the atmosphere, and I knew I was with the only man I would ever love. All the cleverly veiled bitterness of past failed relationships vanished. The scar tissue that threatened to encapsulate my heart daily was suddenly torn away! It was such a relief! I felt unburdened and floating.

I kissed him back intensely and felt the heat bloom inside me! I had worried about how kissing Logan would work, but it all happened perfectly - effortlessly. I could tell he was trembling, which touched me so profoundly.

Logan

Tess gasped in between heated kisses, only stopping to take off my shirt and undo my belt! I was shocked but entirely aroused! Thank the Lord in Heaven I had been working out tenaciously over the last two months, I thought from an old and dying vanity that still clung to me from long ago!

I quickly reciprocated by unbuttoning her shirt, button by button, slowly savoring every one. I spread her comfy flannel to expose the breasts I had pictured a thousand times in my dreams. Her bra was very unassuming but somehow was the sexiest article of clothing I had ever laid eyes on - and I used to date Victoria Secret models!

Tess leaned back, unhooked her bra with a swift, single motion, and let her shirt and bra fall to the floor in unison. My hungry eyes consumed every inch of her while my mind was busy making memories. Her body demanded to be on a canvas, and I wondered if I would be able to finish the current painting before immortalizing this angelic sight!

Quick as a shot came a rush of crippling insecurity! I hadn't been with a woman in over five years! My physique was nowhere near what it had been before, but my belly was gone, and my muscle definition was coming back, so - OH MY GOD!

Was this really what I was thinking about right now of all times!? Get out of your head! I had never been insecure about sex in my life, so the feeling was as alien to me as love. Love! LOVE! I am in love! It's real, and Tess was clearly attracted to me for whatever reason, so I didn't want to waste one more microsecond wondering why!

Reading my mind the way she did, Tess went from a roaring fire to smoldering embers and slowed the pace down a bit. She thoughtfully eased my pants off and had me step out of them. She left my boxers on but took her pants and panties off, revealing herself entirely to me. I was suddenly, and entirely, back in the moment!

Tess

It was so exhilarating to finally break down the wall of wonder with Logan and take the plunge! I was so turned on and anxious to explore him physically that I wanted to slow things down and truly let the experience envelop me - us. I intuited that Logan needed time to gently ease into the moment as well, so I took my time. I wanted this experience to last forever!

To be with a man so strong of spirit yet so delicate and kind was absolutely irresistible. I was so wet with anticipation and already on the verge of climax that I could barely contain myself. It made me realize that the sex I had been having all my life was just a pale, thin representation of what was possible.

Logan looked at me with hunger and happiness. With a fair amount of lust and love. A hundred different emotions registered behind his eyes in the space of one second as he devoured me visually. I had never felt so loved, and, dare I say, I'd never loved so much. Whatever had happened to me in the past, or would happen to me in the future, was irrelevant; this, right now, was the most important time of my life. A time to find true love and happiness. It's all I ever wanted!

Logan stood there before me in nothing but his boxers, and it was my turn to drink him in. He had come so far from the unhealthy, depressed shut-in that I had met a mere two months ago. He was in good shape now, healthy, and really enjoying life outside his comfort zone! He was learning martial arts and getting really good at it!

And his face...his different, unconventional, perfectly imperfect face, was...beautiful. Absolutely beautiful. It was as Natish described but also told such a story.

I truly believe his face saved his soul, and for that, I loved it. Not only because it helped transform him from a spoiled, petty husk to a transcendent, vulnerable man of depth, but because every line, every curve, every texture, every bump represented Logan's journey to being the man he was right then.

I hated the pain he had endured; I loved the pain he had endured - it all led him here to me.

I slinked over to him suggestively and pressed my naked body against his. I could feel him rising beneath his plaid boxers, which drove me mad. I slowly brought them down and marveled at what begged to be inside me. I wanted Logan so bad; I wanted him to love me. I knew he loved me. I loved him. God help me; I loved him.

I led him back to his bedroom, where he gently took me in his arms and kissed me tenderly. Strange how each kiss seemed to reach deep and stoke my desire. I ruffled his hair with my hands while he massaged my body, breasts, and finally...

The moment he touched me between my legs, I climaxed. Not explosively, but sweetly, softly, gently, in a way that was so gratifying.

Logan

Tess, now lying down on my bed, drew a desperate breath in as I touched her. Suddenly, she was a voracious fire once again! I dove into those flames and let them engulf me. Love was the fire in which I now burned.

It was fascinating the differences between sex with someone you love and sex with someone you don't. It was night and day. I had been living my whole life in order to get to this point, and now that I was here, I knew I hadn't been living at all.

A flood of passion and emotion overwhelmed my mind and body as she invited me inside. Slowly, I entered her and felt my soul sing. I never wanted something so badly in my life. If I was unworthy, I didn't care.

All of my senses came together suddenly; the feel of being inside her, the smell of her rosehips and avocado lotion, the sound of her gasping for air, and the taste of her salty skin. I had to hold myself back from climaxing; It was all so overwhelming!

It was like my first time, and I wanted to explore every millimeter of her flesh for eternity. There were gentle kisses that turned ravenous. There were escalating peaks and valleys of sensation; each peak was more intense than the last, and each valley a tender respite. My hands were no longer my own, guided by some inner force that compelled me to read her curves and lines with every receptor.

I rode her like a wave rides the beach and followed her every subtle body movement like a blueprint. It was like picking up a violin for the first time and having the strings show you how to play Beethoven.

In an instant, Tess rolled me to the bottom and took over! She was on top of me, drenching me in her sweat and sex. She tangled me up in her hair, and it felt like a hundred butterflies kissing my face as she stared down into my eyes. As if my eyes had begged her, she descended and kissed me hard with soft lips. I lost myself in her eyes and that kiss.

Tess

Logan's skilled lovemaking was enrapturing! He read my every movement like an instruction manual and did everything my body wanted, even before my mind knew I wanted it!

It wasn't just his skill and physical intuition that was so sensual; it was also his soul. Such kindness, wisdom, and reflection resided within him. I didn't care what he had done in the past; he was a new man.

His hands were always at the right place on my body at the right time, touching all my hot spots the moment they lit up. He kissed me so artfully and passionately, truly better than anyone with picture-perfect lips ever had. His body was gorgeous, even if he wasn't as sculpted as he had been before, his strong arms held me tight and tenderly, and those hips worked his cute ass like a gymnast.

His rhythm never left me wanting! He was constantly moving me towards a climax and never hit any stops.

His cock was the perfect size and shape to keep pressure on my pleasure centers. Every thrust and every withdrawal had me seizing with gratification. I instinctively met his hips with my own, slapping his thighs with mine, crying out in ecstasy!

I was biting my lip so hard that I thought for certain I would draw blood! His head was nuzzled next to mine, his ear to my mouth, savoring all my moans and throaty whispers. He kissed my neck and sent shivers up my spine that felt like little lizards running up and down my back.

His hands moved from my breasts to my ass as he suddenly spun me underneath him again. His positioning and leverage were exquisite; I opened my legs wide and succumbed to multiple orgasms! I drenched his cock as the climaxes continued to outpace one another, each one becoming more intense than the last until I reached a crescendo that was life affirming!

I went supernova! My back arched, my legs locked, my arms turned to jelly, and I couldn't stop myself from crying out, screaming my release!

I had to taste myself on him to confirm this was reality and not some fever dream. I immediately went down on him, putting him entirely in my mouth. The mixture of salty sweetness was electrifying! The charge of my climax, still dripping down his dick, hit my tongue like a 9-volt-battery!

He suddenly exploded inside my mouth, mixing his cum with my own, and that was enough to send me into climax all over again! I drank him down as I played with myself. I came again and naturally thought that was the finale, but I was so wrong.

Logan

The moment she went down on me after cumming on my cock, I knew I would not be able to hold myself back! I let the most intense orgasm I have ever experienced leave me like a bullet from a barrel.

Tess used her tongue to pull every last drop from my sensitive tip as I writhed and hyperventilated. Typically, this would have been the point where we both rolled over joyfully, exhausted and spent; however, I was nowhere near done!

I reciprocated by going down on her, and I can say with no bias that she tasted like a peach. When I was certain she had cum again, I raised up, and without a word, she rolled over and stuck her perfect ass into the air. I needed no invitation and slowly entered her from behind. I could tell right away that this position was a finisher for both of us!

We both climaxed again in unison, then crumpled like two weary fighters. Tess found the strength to hoist herself up and lay on my chest.

"So, I guess I ***haven't*** been having sex all these years," Tess said breathlessly.

"Noooooo doubt." I managed. "Wow.

Chapter Seven

The Next Morning

Tess

Typically, when I woke up alongside a man the next morning, I was fretful. What if he changes? What if this is a mistake? What if I got myself into something toxic? What if he doesn't really like me? What if I don't really like him? What if, what if, what if...

This morning, my "what if" voice was blissfully quiet. There was a certainty that hung in the air. A reality that was undeniable. I. WAS. IN. LOVE!!!!!!!

The lovemaking had gone on most of the night and was something so special that I knew I would cherish the memory for all my days. Logan was an incredible lover! I had never experienced such lusty and fulfilling sex in my life, but it was the emotional and spiritual connection that embellished the experience beyond description. Everything felt right. Everything felt in place.

The sun filtered in through a gap in the curtains and illuminated the millions of lazy dust particles suspended in the air. That's exactly how I felt; like I was floating, basking in the light of something deeply special.

I cuddled up to Logan and held him tight, never wanting to let him go.

Logan

I woke up to Tess holding me tight, and I simply couldn't allow myself to believe that this was reality. It was too good to be true. I had never done anything worthy of this reprieve. All this time, I considered my condition as retribution for my misdeeds, a grotesque, physical representation of my heart; punishment for my vanity, my diabolical nature, my greed, my selfishness...

But now, I look at it in a completely different way. My condition was my salvation! It saved my life, my soul and led me to my greatest love.

I held her tight, stroked her hair, and thanked my lucky stars.

Tess turned to me and smiled brighter than the ribbon of sun slicing through the curtain. "Good morning," she whispered into my ear.

"It is indeed!" I proclaimed! "I think we need to have a celebratory, cheat-day breakfast!"

"Oh no you don't! You're not using my sweet lovin' as an excuse to eat a pound of bacon,” Tess playfully scolded. "You get two slices, along with your egg-white omelet, like every morning!"

"Ahhhh, but ma!" I said through faux tears. "Okay, okay. But instead of martial arts training this morning..." I coyly started with a wink.

"Mmmmmmmm, now you're talkin'," Tess said in a sexy, low voice.

She climbed on top of me, straddling my lap, and began kissing me softly. After a moment, she began moving down my chest. In an instant, I was inside her mouth.

I had never before told a person I loved them and meant it, but the words were fighting to escape my lips. I wouldn't let them; there was no need to rush this or risk spoiling the natural process.

When Tess and I finally got out of bed and had breakfast, she reminded me of my surgery, scheduled a few weeks from now. I was really dreading it, but not near as much as the task I was to carry out next week. I had tracked John down and planned to go see him.

Tess was uneasy about my going to see him only a week before my surgery, but I was determined. I emailed John the week prior and was surprised to see he responded the next day.

He was chilly and curt with his response but had agreed to meet with me. He forwarded me his address and phone number and politely wished us safe travels. It was encouraging, but I began bracing myself for the very real possibility that he would not forgive me. Moreover, he may have some pretty hard words for me. In any case, I felt we both needed closure. In many ways, this was selfishly more for me than him, but I couldn't shake the feeling it needed to be done. Tess also felt it was for the best and agreed to go with me.

Her support and presence were so vital. I promised myself I wouldn't depend on her to shoulder the weight of every little problem in my life but having her in my orbit just embellished me. I understood the importance of maintaining a level of independence and not spoiling things by forging a codependent relationship chemistry, but I'm fairly certain Tess wouldn't fall for that anyway. She kicked my butt on the regular to ensure I was always venturing outside of my comfort zone.

Initially, I wanted to charter a private flight down to South Carolina, but Tess thought driving the 12 hours there would give me time to work through what I wanted to say and prepare myself emotionally. I agreed, so we decided to rent a nice SUV to take us. When we started actually making plans, my stomach began fluttering with the reality of what I was doing. I had to be strong.

Tess

I was really proud of Logan for deciding to go see John. It was going to be a difficult meeting and would most likely open up old wounds, but it seemed like the right thing to do. I was actually looking forward to the trip.

I started putting a list together of things we would need when my cell phone rang. It was Natish calling!

"Hey, girl! How are you!?" I asked cheerfully.

"I dunno, Tess. My spider sense is tingling," Natish said tensely.

"Oh no, what's up!?" I could feel dread creeping up on me, like in the old days.

"Well, I was jogging past your house just now, and I saw the same black SUV, with tinted windows, parked outside your house that I've seen parked outside of mine. I know this for certain because I recognize the license plate." Natish's voice was solemn and urgent, completely different from her normal confident, jovial tone. "I'm coming around the back of your house now; let me in."

"Okay, I'm headed to the gate now..." My pleasant, peaceful morning had clouds threatening the horizon.

I raced out the back door to the rear gate, and Natish was already there.

"Hey honey, I'm sorry to put your dander up like this, but something is definitely up with that SUV." Natish looked nervously back and forth as she came inside the yard. I slammed the back gate and locked it.

"No! We really appreciate you looking out for us!" My stomach had knots now.

We quickly ran into the house, and Natish led me to the edge of the front window. We both went to either side and peered through the curtains. Sure enough, there was a black SUV parked across the street.

"You're sure that's the same one from your house," I asked pensively.

"I'm sure, doll. Definitely the same motherfucker." Natish was tense and ready to snap. "I didn't think too much of it until I saw it outside your house just now. I jogged by them twice last week and, by luck, happened to notice the license plate. Say's Be Ryce. Yeah, it's that clown again."

"Ohhh shit," I said, my heart sinking. "I should have known he wouldn't go quietly."

"Oh, he's gonna go!" Natish barked, her anxiety now replaced by anger. "That twerpy fuckin' honkey motherf - sorry!"

"Yeah, no, you're spot on. What should we do?!" I cried out! Here was my worst, most terrible baggage washing up on shore, threatening my dear friend, her family, and my sweet Logan.

"I'll tell you what *I'm* gonna do: *I'm* gonna get Furious over here right now, with a couple hard-hittin' ma'fuckers to put a hurtin' on homeboy out there!" Natish growled while forcefully poking the buttons on her cell phone. "Motherfucker gonna try and threaten mine and MY people - oh HEEEEELLLLLLL NO!"

I didn't know if I should be more afraid of Bryce or what Natish might do *to* Bryce!

Right then, Logan rounded the corner with a towel wrapped around his head like Lucile Ball, "Hey, Natish! Great to -" But before Logan could enunciate his words, Natish grabbed him by the arm and directed him behind her!

"Hey, Logan! Don't move!?" Natish ordered, her phone plastered to her head.

Logan looked at me and signed with his hands, "What the Hell is going on!?"

I signed back, "Looks like," my hands faltered, so I whispered, "Bryce" and finished the rest with sign language, "is out front stalking the house!"

Logan's eyes darkened, and he moved to the hallway closet with stealthy ease. In a flash, he had a pump-action shotgun in his hands and racked a shell into the chamber. "I was hoping I'd get another chance with that fucker," Logan said, his practiced speech now degenerating into barely intelligible words.

"Hold that thought, Logan," Natish ordered, holding out her arm to restrain him. "Hey honey, where are the kids?...Oh, they're with Nanny? Good! Are Mike and Cannon still with you?...Excellent! That fuckin' Elton John lookin' motherfucker from the BBQ is parked out front of Logan and Tess's house. AND, I just figured out it's the same damn SUV that's been parked outside of our house!...Yeah, right now...Yeah I'm sure!...Alright, we'll stay inside until you get here."

Natish, still holding Logan back, whispered to us both, "Furious and his boys are on the way!"

"Um, shouldn't we have called the police?" Tess asked sheepishly.

"The police!? Hell na," Natish said confidently. "We wanna scare 'em and let them know that we know they're scoping us. Only thing cops are gonna do is harass Furious and me for being black in a white-ass neighborhood."

Logan and I both nodded our heads; she was right.

"We don't want any trouble- " I started to say, but Natish cut me off.

"Them parking outside our homes is trouble enough. If we call the cops, they'll just go away and come back later. We need to send a message. Don't worry, ain't nobody going to shoot anyone...unless Doc Holiday here starts spraying buckshot."

Logan huffed, put the shotgun down, and peeked out from behind the curtain overtop Natish.

Suddenly, from behind the black SUV, we could see Furious and two of his huge friends creeping up with baseball bats.

My heart was in my throat, and I was really rattled! Furious hunkered underneath the backseat window on the driver's side and prepared to pounce. Mike and Cannon were posted low behind the rearview window and the passenger-side window.

Suddenly, Furious jumped to his feet and swung the bat like Vladimir Guerrero Jr. right at the driver's window! It exploded in a barrage of safety glass and exposed Bryce's astonished and bewildered face!

Taking a cue from Furious, Mike and Cannon both started blasting the SUV with their bats, smashing windows and denting metal! Two of Bryce's entourage were so startled they froze in place!

Furious reached into the driver's side window and started pulling Bryce out into the street! Fortunately for Bryce, he still had his seatbelt on, so Furious couldn't get him through the opening. Bryce fumbled but managed to hit the vehicle's start button and fired up the engine.

Furious grabbed hold of his coat and started screaming, "Yeah, that's right ma'fucker! I got you now!"

Bryce stomped the gas and squealed off in a cloud of burned rubber, leaving Furious clutching the lapel of Bryce's glittery jacket!

"Fuck!" Furious shouted in anger while his buddies were laughing their asses off. Furious ran up to the house, and we already had the door open. "I'm sorry, baby, I couldn't get him through the window! You guys all okay!?"

Natish laughing now, "It's okay, my love; I think he got the message!"

"No, he didn't," Furious stated, his words rife with angst. "This motherfucker will definitely be back with all kinds of trouble. We better circle the wagons."

I was mortified! I couldn't believe it was my douchebag ex-boyfriend who was causing so much trouble again! Not just for me but the people I loved and cared about.

"Should we call the cops now?" I asked again.

Furious thought on it for a moment... "Honestly, *FUCK!* - I think we better. We need to get in front of this. Technically, we just assaulted *them*. Tess, would you mind calling them? We'll get our story straight while we wait."

"I'll call them right now," I said, still shaken.

"Tess, you and Logan stay close," Furious demanded, "we'll need your whiteness." Suddenly, we all burst out laughing.

"Okay, okay, fools! Stop laughing!" Natish demanded.

Logan

Once Tess called the cops, we huddled up in the living room to talk about what we would say. Since Bryce tried to kidnap Tess and was a wannabe gangster, he probably had some kind of criminal history. That, coupled with the altercation at Natish and Furious's BBQ, gave us ample reason to fear for our lives.

We would just explain to the cops that Natish had seen Bryce's SUV outside their house twice, not knowing it was him. She didn't connect the dots until she saw him posted outside our house while jogging. She remembered him from the BBQ and called Furious. Fearing for his wife and friends, Furious came running, armed with a baseball bat. Upon confronting Bryce, Furious felt threatened and reacted. It was all legitimate; we just wanted to get our story straight.

Furious told Mike and Cannon to get out of there before the police arrived, and he would handle everything. They obliged without a shove.

I felt weird about having to tell our whole story to the cops, but what else were we going to do? It was all true and painted a dark picture of Bryce and his boys. I started to hope that maybe we could get Bryce locked up if he wasn't smart enough to go away.

When the police finally arrived - 3 hours later - we had our story straight. The cops were aware of Bryce and his activity in the area, which was a huge help to us. Apparently, he was mixed up in human trafficking, among other illicit activities, and Tess was extremely lucky to have escaped him and his crew. According to them, a lot of missing girls in the tri-state area have been linked to Bryce and his crew. Apparently, they had ties to the Russian mob, which didn't go a long way in alleviating our concern.

They made a report and promised to have units drive by both our houses regularly, but we were warned to be extremely careful. Furious and Natish had to bite their tongues respectfully but were clearly skeptical of the police doing anything that would help us.

When the cops were pulling away, we all went inside for a much needed drink. I broke out the good stuff and poured everyone a double snifter.

Furious took a sniff, then a taste, "Wow, Logan. You, sir, know your scotch."

"You're damn right," I said with a chuckle. I turned to Tess and signed while I spoke in a breathy, more composed voice, "I'm guessing we should hold off on our trip next week?"

"Yeah, I guess so. I'm so sorry, Logan. I know how important it was to you," Tess said in a quiet, distracted tone.

"It's fine!" I said. "We'll put it off until after the surgery. Probably just as well."

That didn't sit very well with Natish, "No, you two go. Mike and Cannon can watch your place. We'll keep in contact to make sure no one is misbehaving at either house."

"Mike and Cannon are really good people, so you don't have to worry about anything," Furious reassured us. "They will take good care of your place, and you'll never even know they were here."

"Are you sure!?" I asked.

"Absolutely," Furious and Natish said in unison.

"I can pay them -" I began, but Furious cut me off.

"No, sir. Won't hear of it," Furious said firmly. "Seriously, they won't mind one bit. You both are family, just like them."

"Well, if they ever need us to watch their house because of human trafficking, Russian mobsters, we'll be more than happy to!" Tess proclaimed. "I'm so sorry, everyone. This is all my fault."

We all turned our heads towards Tess and tilted them in unison, the way she always did.

"Okay, okay! I get it," Tess said, laughing while choking back tears. "I love you all so much! You're the best family I never had."

"Family takes care of family," I said.

"Damn right," Furious confirmed.

Chapter Eight

You First

Logan

The day finally arrived for Tess and I to take our trip down south. I was dealing with a lot of emotions that morning, but I knew this was something I had to do.

I was confident leaving the house with Mike and Cannon was a smart move. They were both former marines, who were hard as Hell and carved out of wood; not to mention they were two of the nicest people I've ever met. I kept falling all over myself, thanking everyone for their help. Mike and Cannon never once got irritated at having to reassure me that it was perfectly fine; they would text with updates, and make sure to hold the fort.

Tess and I left them a freezer full of their favorite foods, thanks to a shopping list provided by Natish and Furious. I pointed them to my private cache of whiskey, single-malt scotch, and medicinal cannabis - to which they were genuinely grateful. I also notified the police that they would be watching the house and gave them carte blanche to do whatever they felt was necessary while they were guests in our house. "Our house," the thought tickled me. Maybe one day it would be ours.

Tess talked with Natish, while the guys and I finished packing up the rental SUV. I made sure to get the biggest, nicest, most comfortable SUV I could find, so we could spread out during the trek. I figured I'd probably have to stop for gas every 15 minutes, but I like a big vehicle when doing a long drive.

When we were all set to go, we spent 45 minutes trying to say goodbye to everyone. We were only going for 5 days, but I felt like we were blasting off into space the way we carried on. It was really sweet and made me feel like I was part of a family, something I had never experienced before in my life. I got the feeling Tess felt the same way.

After I told them all to be careful and alert for the millionth time, we hugged, waved goodbye, and we were on our way!

I was so thrilled to have Tess with me on this journey. Not just the journey to South Carolina, but the journey of our lives. Our bond had become so tight I couldn't imagine myself without her.

We were like decades old friends. We didn't fight, we didn't get in each other's way, and we didn't feel the need to be on top of one another. While we didn't like a lot of the same TV shows or movies, we always compromised. That right there, in and of itself, told me we were soul mates. If two people can compromise over television, they can compromise over anything.

Oftentimes, I would paint while she watched some obscure, low-budget horror movie (which I hate to admit,

I'm kind of getting into). We were together most of the time, but it never felt like too much.

I was very close to finishing the painting of the BBQ, which was one of my fondest memories. I promised Tess I wouldn't sell it, much to Natish's chagrin. I promised Natish and Furious that I would paint something very special for them but also gave them the painting in my dining room that Natish loved so much.

Natish was chomping at the bit to be my agent as well, and I would be a fool not to let her. I hadn't told her I had decided to take her on yet because I wanted to surprise her after we got back. She had blown me away a few days prior with all the knowledge and savvy she had compiled surrounding the art industry through skillful, diligent and careful research. Natish was a hard-edged professional with such poise and panache that I couldn't help but be impressed! Not to mention she was a pit bull! Her plan for my return to the art world was absolutely brilliant. She was truly an artist herself.

Tess dozed off during the first leg of our trip, and I had a hard time keeping my eyes on the road and not her.

I hated driving more than anything, which is why I avoided it as much as possible. I just didn't have the patience for it. I get very angry at other drivers and their stupidity. I start tailgating, taking unnecessary risks, and screaming at people. If a disfigured man was ever screaming at you in traffic, it was probably me.

We were only an hour into our trip, and my road rage was already heating up. I started growling and cursing under my breath, trying not to wake Tess up. Naturally, every dipshit in the world was directly in front of me, in the fast lane, slow racing every other dipshit in the world in the right lane.

"Oh, for fuck sake!!" I hollered before I could stifle it.

Tess popped one eye open and looked at me. "I thought you might need this..." she said in a drowsy tone as she fished a joint out of her shirt pocket.

"Nice! Will you be joining me?" I asked in my best voice.

"No, I ate a few gummies, so I'm gooooooood!" Tess gave me the shooter hand signal and pulled the imaginary hammer with her thumb while clicking her tongue. "Oh wait, lemme put a cherry on top of that for you..." Tess pulled out her phone, queued up some old-school hip-hop and let it rip over the stereo. "You're welcome," she said, blowing me kisses.

I had never listened to hip-hop before in my life, but I have to say, I quite enjoyed it. I didn't know who the musician was, but the combination of gritty Jamaican lyrics, a pounding bass, and a rare, but a resplendent combination of beats, put me right in the mood. I fired up the jay and puffed, traffic all but forgotten now!

"Don't get pulled over," Tess warned from behind closed eyes.

"Don't worry about it!" I said and pinched her boob.

"Don't start something you can't finish, pal," Tess said dreamily as she slipped back into sleep.

Now, this was living! Cruising down the road, listening to the radio, puffing a jay, my sweet baby in the passenger side - who was I? I didn't recognize myself anymore, and I had never been happier.

After a couple of hours of driving, I needed a break, some fuel, and some munchies. Haha, "munchies." I couldn't believe I hadn't been fully utilizing my medicinal cannabis more frequently! Up until now, I would only puff a little and go straight to bed, but this was like floating down the road on a moving couch, my problems struggling to keep up. I had some crazy ideas for paintings and wanted to really deep-dive into old-school hip-hop as soon as I possibly could!

Tess stirred as I pulled into the off-ramp, made a right, and drove into the gas station next to a pump. "Hey, can you get me some Funyuns and a soda? I'll take over driving for a bit."

"Absolutely! I'll be right back."

"Wait, you forgot this..." Tess reeled me in and gave me a big kiss. "There, you may go now."

"How could I have forgotten that?" I said with some effort. Damn masses in my mouth were really starting to piss me off. I hadn't bothered talking for so long, and now I was talking all the time. I couldn't wait to get these lipomas removed so I could speak more easily.

"I'll get out and pump the gas," Tess said, stretching.

"You're the best!" I said, humming a beat from one of the hip-hop tracks as I went inside the convenience store.

As soon as I walked inside, there were three sets of wide, male, rugged eye's gawking at me. Gotta love rural West Virginia! "Hey, fellas," I said, walking by waving. They were too stunned to reply, but at least one of them raised his hand in a bewildered wave.

It was hard to believe a few months ago I would have rather been eaten alive by fire ants than step one foot inside a convenience store full of good 'ole boys, but here I was. And I wasn't even that worked up over it! I simply didn't care anymore.

I grabbed a ton of snacks now that my buzz was waning and my hunger was kicking in. I scooped up donuts, chips, candy bars, sodas, and, of course, Funyuns. I could barely carry everything up to the counter without dropping it all.

"Well, someone's got the munchies," the older, grizzled clerk joked.

"It's my cheat day," I said jovially without missing a beat.

"Um hmmm! Either you hit a skunk out there on the road, or you been settin' fire to the Devil's lettuce!" With that, all three of the men began to guffaw.

I couldn't help but join them in laughter. "Well, a road trip without weed ain't much of a road trip, indeed!"

That really set them off, and they were suddenly laughing big, barrel-chested laughs. One guy actually took his cowboy hat off and swatted his butt, "Now ain't that about the damn truth!"

The other fella who waved spoke up, "Be careful rollin' outta town; the Sheriff has been on the warpath lately. He likes them out 'a state plates too."

"Thanks, I appreciate the heads up!" I was delighted at how nice they were.

"You betcha!" He said, smiling a cigarette stained smile.

"That'll be fifty-four bucks with the gas, brother," the clerk said, grinning genuinely. "Well, oh shit. Your party's about to be pooped," he grumbled while making change. His two buddies looked out the window, and all the fun left the room.

"Oh man," the older cowboy said mournfully while tucking his head back inside his hat. "That's a disappointment. You better get out there and get your lady-friend inside the car before Randy man-handles her to death."

I followed their gazes out the dusty, cracked window and put my eyes on Randy. He was a hulking, dirty, brazen old boy with a jagged smile and fifteen hands. He was pushing up on Tess with a complete disregard for personal space. I could tell she was trying to be polite, but she looked rattled!

"Thanks, guys," I said, collecting my bag full of goodies. "Best go die standin' up."

"Holler if you need me to call the Sheriff!" The clerk yelled after me.

I tipped my imaginary cowboy hat to them and scuttled out the door. Tess never looked so happy to see me. She was basically using soft martial arts to slap Randy's hands away from her tits and ass.

I raised my voice to him, "Well, what do we have here? Shouldn't you be finding some flowers for Algernon?"

"What the fuck's it to you -" He started, full of bravado, but naturally, his voice, thick with accent, trailed off as he laid eyes on my face. "Wellllllll Hooooollleeeeee shit! Will ya lookit you!?"

"Please do," I said cordially. "It's an honor when folks marvel at the way God made me."

"God ain't got nuthin' to do with that face, partner." He said, swaggering towards me and away from Tess, which was exactly my plan.

"Tomato, to-mah-toe," I said light-heartedly.

"Whatever, fuck face. Me and the lady here are having a conversation, and you ain't invited."

"Actually, that's the love of my life you're trying to have a conversation with there, Randy," I spoke these words more clearly than anything I've spoken to date.

"How the fuck do you know my name!?" Randy demanded, cracking his knuckles. He was now standing over me like a civil war statue.

"I'm a warlock. In exchange for magical powers I had to sacrifice my good looks."

"The fuck, you say! This is your last chance..." Randy said, driving his point home by pounding his finger into my chest. Jesus H. Hillbilly Cornbread Christ, are all dipshits the same?

I grabbed his fingers, just like I did Bryce, turned them up to the sky, kicked his weight leg, and put him down on his knee. He hollered out like a polecat and grabbed his elbow. "Owwwwwww!!!"

I held him there for a long moment, letting the situation sink in. I hate to admit that I was loving every second of this. "Now, Randy, I can completely understand your wanting to chat up an angel like my Tess there, but it's ungentlemanly to get handsy with a lady who isn't interested. Furthermore, I'm not mad at you; I just think you need to consider others more intently in the future."

"FUCK YOU -!" Randy bellowed and tried to break the hold I had on him.

"Now, now. What did I say about being more gentlemanly?" I tightened my hold and forced him back to his knee. "The only crime here is not learning the lesson."

"I'm...I'm sorry," Randy said, actually tearing up.

"It's okay. Apologize to the lady, and we can forget all about this unpleasantness."

Randy turned his head to face Tess, who was now standing to his right with her arms crossed and a very pointed frown.

"I'm sorry, ma'am! You're just pretty, is all," Randy blubbered.

Tess sighed, pulled a joint out of her pocket, and put it in Randy's top shirt pocket. "No harm, no foul. If you are polite and cordial, girls will talk to you. Be nice and kind; that's the secret." Tess patted his pocket, "That's to remind you to relax and be well, Randy."

The clerk, cowboy, and cowboy's friend came rushing out to get a better look at what was going on.

The clerk spoke first, "Randy, I called the Sheriff, so you better behave yourself and stop pestering my customers!"

Randy looked over to the clerk with a mixture of anger and humiliation, "Screw you, Hank! This ma'fucker's got me in the kung-fu grip!"

The cowboy spoke next, "Get yourself together boy and get your ass back to work. Your momma taught you better'n this!"

Now I spoke, "I'm going to let you go, Randy. If you try to get handsy *with me*, I'm going to kung-fu your ass all up and down main street. Understood?"

"Uh-huh," Randy said, sniffling.

"Okay then..." I released his hand, which he jerked quickly away, and stood up.

Tess and I quickly made our way to the SUV and climbed inside while Randy massaged his hand and wrist. "Motherfuckers! This shit ain't over!"

At that exact moment, the Sheriff pulled in nonchalantly behind Randy, who hadn't noticed. The Sheriff rolled his window down to speak to Randy, but the greasy goon was still yelling at us. "I'm coming right behind you, fuck face! And I'm bringing my shotgun with me! We'll see how uppity you are with a gun barrel up your ass!"

I pulled the SUV up next to Randy and the Sheriff, whom he still hadn't seen. "Afternoon, Sheriff. In addition to threatening to kill us, you might want to check his upper shirt pocket."

Randy spun around to see the Sheriff looking right at him. "Wha-, well, hey Sheriff!"

The Sheriff sighed a great sigh, "Hello, Randy. Why don't you empty your pockets out on the hood of my car before I yank a knot in you so tight you'll have two assholes." Randy, all the hot air leaving his sails, reached into his shirt pocket and dropped the joint on the hood of the Sheriff's car.

"They put it in my pocket, Sheriff! I swear!" Randy said, tears threatening again.

"I'm sure they did, son," the Sheriff said sarcastically. He turned his gaze to us, " You folks go on and have a nice day. Sorry about this one here; he's a poor representation of our town."

"No worries. It's still a beautiful town." I said in my best polite citizen voice.

"Well, thank you. Y'all take care," the Sheriff said, exiting his vehicle.

"We will! And thank you!" We waved as we drove off while the Sheriff put Randy up against the car and frisked him.

When we were a safe distance away, Tess and I looked at one another and burst out laughing.

"Well, I think that went the way it was supposed to," Tess said, giggling.

"I'll tell you one thing," I began, the adrenaline dying off, "I'm never complaining about martial arts training again."

"Pffffffft, yeah, yeah, you'll be crying about it tomorrow morning," Tess promised matter-of-factly.

"Well, it seems we only need to know the one move," I said jokingly. "I guess it's written somewhere in the asshole's handbook to just walk up and start poking people in the chest."

"Lucky for us," Tess said, triggering another bout of laughter.

"Shit, from now on, I'll pump the gas, and you go get the snacks."

"No doubt," Tess agreed, leaning in to give me a kiss on the cheek. "My hero!"

"Don't you mean Randy's hero? I'm pretty sure if I hadn't intervened, you would have torn his arms off and beat him to death with them."

"You're not wrong..." Tess said slyly, a smile creeping up on her lips.

As we continued down the road, Tess was getting squirmy. "I'm bored; let's play a game!"

I turned the music down, "Okay, what would you like to play?"

"I dunno, I can't think of anything," Tess said, laughing.

"Me either! Tell me about your childhood. You know, when you were growing up," I proposed.

Tess's demeanor changed a little as a solemn sadness wrapped itself around her. "I'd hate to bring the party down," she half-whispered. "It's not one of those feel good Hallmark movie stories." She tried to laugh and lighten the mood, but it fell short.

"Well, I can relate. We have another 10 hours, so I'll tell you my life story if you tell me yours." I offered her the best version of a smile I could muster.

"I love your smile," Tess said, brightening again. "Okay, but you first!"

"It would be my pleasure." It wasn't a pleasure, of course, but I wanted her to know everything about me, and I her.

She had already seen me at my worst, so a little context wouldn't hurt things. I was certain there was nothing she could say that would make me feel differently about her.

So, I went first. We had shared a lot over the last couple of months, but I had glossed over good old Uncle Effram and his icy eccentricities, as well as pulling that kid's pinky nail out. Talking about boarding school and going to the Les Beaux Arts de Paris, traveling, et cetera, proved much easier to talk about. Tess was captivated by my stories, but after a while, I had to stop; I was really struggling with talking this much. My mouth was exhausted, and my tongue was starting to hurt.

Tess finally offered a reprieve, "I guess it's my turn." She reflected momentarily, "You've led such an interesting but lonesome life, Logan. Not so dissimilar from my own."

Chapter Nine

Tess, Just Tess

Tess

"I grew up in Florida. My mother, Chloe, was French, married an ex-marine named Robert Peterson, whom she met while he was stationed in France. After the wedding, they moved to Miami, Florida. I was an only child, an accident, born late in their marriage." As I began telling Logan about my childhood, my mind picked over all the salty details. Logan had been candid with me, so I would be candid with him.

"After my father murdered my mother and killed himself, I dropped Peterson as a last name. Now I'm Tess...Just Tess." Logan stiffened when I told him about my mother and father, but that was to be expected.

Logan's upbringing was all about his uncle using separation and isolation to manage him, whereas mine was all about my father using fear and domination to control my mother and I.

My father was an unbelievable bastard. He drank too much, he smoked too much, he cursed too much, and he was always angry. He was obsessed with controlling every facet of my mother's life, but I suspect she wanted to be controlled. When I was born, his obsession grew to encompass me as well, but I would not be controlled.

My mother blamed me for upsetting the equation of their relationship, which is to say, she was fine being oppressed by a tyrant husband.

When I came along and refused to reside under his thumb, the beatings came for both of us. My mother loved me dearly, but I knew she resented me for standing up for myself the way she never could and creating problems.

They would run off for days at a time, leaving me alone in a filthy, uncared for home. I had to fend for myself through much of my adolescent years. I had to get myself to school, I had to get a job to pay for food, and I had to pay most of the bills. Fortunately, the house was already paid for, but it was a tiny, decomposing, dilapidated old house that was steadily sinking into a Florida swamp.

I had no extended family, but my neighbors were really nice. They grasped the situation I was in and were always dropping off goodie bags with groceries and essentials to help me out. Mr. Petrillo and his wife, an elderly couple in their eighties, lived right next door and were especially nice to me. They were all leery of my father, however, which constantly kept me at arm's length with them. I had a few friends that were in similar situations, but they were all about partying and screwing around. I wanted to graduate, go to culinary school and make something of myself as a chef.

When I was 17, my mother finally had enough. She was sick of us being punching bags, felt terrible about the relationship between her and I, and wanted to try and do right by me. She wanted me to go to culinary school almost as bad as I wanted to go!

Mom told me of her plan to leave dad, take the savings, disappear, and put me through culinary school. I was ecstatic!

She said it would just be the two of us from that point forward! After weeks of planning and preparation, the night finally came for us to leave. My mother gave me a cashier's check for twelve thousand dollars, their entire life savings, and told me to wait at the bus station. She would meet me there, but if anything happened and she wasn't there by midnight, I was to take the bus North to Pensacola, Florida, and wait for her. If she didn't arrive within a day, I was on my own.

I was terrified but also excited. I was almost 18 and had grown up fast, so I felt like I could handle it. Above everything, I was scared for my mother.

I sat at the bus station until 2 am, and that's when I saw my father storming in through the front entrance. There was no running or hiding; I was right there up front where he could see me, on one of the benches. He marched directly up to me, grabbed my arm and started dragging me towards the front door. There was no one really around, just a ticket agent in the booth who pretended not to see us.

I fought him tooth and nail, but he forced me into his old Chevy truck and took off towards home. I didn't say a word, and I didn't cry, but I was already planning my escape.

When we got home, and he stopped the truck, I tried to run, but he caught me and dragged me kicking and screaming back to the house. Once inside, I could see my mother lying slumped on the floor, bruised and beaten. I couldn't tell if she was unconscious or dead.

My father sat me down hard on a creaky wooden chair. He stared into my eyes from five inches away for a long moment. He demanded to know where the money was. I acted like I had no idea what he was saying, and he slapped me hard across the mouth.

He threatened to kill my mother if I didn't tell him where the money was. I remained tight-lipped until he stomped over to where she lay and snatched her up. She stirred, so she was still alive.

At that point, my father clapped both hands around her throat and started to squeeze with all his might, all the while looking at me and demanding to know where the money was. I finally relented and held up the cashier's check. He dropped my mother to the floor like a sack of potatoes and quickly moved to grab the check.

He snatched it out of my hand, smacked me again, and told me that sneaky bitches like us deserved what we got. He crossed the floor back to where my mother was and placed his boot on her neck. I could tell he was standing on her with his full weight while she weakly fought.

I started crying and pleading with him to stop, but he continued to crush her throat. Suddenly, I heard a wet snap, and my mother went completely limp. I screamed bloody murder as he made his way back over to me, promising I was next.

A loud voice calling from outside quickly startled us to attention! It was our neighbor, Mr. Petrillo! My father's face twisted into an angry rictus as he clenched his fists and hollered out for him to get the Hell off his property. Before Mr. Petrillo could respond, the yard was suddenly flooded with police.

My father froze in his tracks, illuminated with blue and red flashing lights that made him look like a horror movie slasher. He suddenly looked at me with such contempt and disdain I thought he would kill me with his eyes alone. Instead, he crumpled up the check, threw it in my face, stormed into the bedroom, and slammed the door!

As the cops began banging on the door, I heard the shot from the bedroom! Naturally, he took the coward's way out. The cops exploded through the front entrance at that point and rushed every corner of our crumbling home. There was only me, sitting there crying - a total mess.

There in my lap, looking like trash, was the cashier's check. I quickly stuffed it into my pants pocket and let a female officer rush me out of there.

I was in a foster home for the next 8 months while I aged out. When I turned 18, I was on my own. Fortunately, I was able to save the cashier's check, and the first thing I did when I left foster care was move to New York, open a bank account, and get a crappy apartment in the Bronx. I used the remainder of the check to enroll in culinary school, and I was able to secure a job at a respectable restaurant.

Over the last 15 years, I've had a lot of ups and downs in the culinary world. My big break was getting the sous-chef job at Totonno's in New York. Unfortunately, the pandemic scuttled that ship. Nevertheless, everything happens for a reason, and I would have traveled that same road a million times because it led to Logan.

Chapter Ten

The Undeniably Awkward Interactions of Men

Logan

I was incredibly shocked and terribly saddened to hear about Tess's parents. I had never been so glad mine just disappeared. I suppose no matter how bad you think you have it, someone else will always have it worse. It made me shudder to think of those who had it worse than Tess. I had to push away the feelings of guilt for thinking my past was so awful when others have had it so much worse than I. Our personal prisons will always seem the worst to us because we are the ones locked inside them.

I felt like I finally knew all of Tess's different facets, and she mine. We stopped for the night in order to get some rest before meeting with John the next day. Tess and I held one another for hours in silence as the sun set fantastically behind the hotel window.

I may not have been able to convince Tess to fly there privately, but she didn't give much push back when I booked us a really nice suite at the Hyatt in Charlotte, NC. We settled in, got cleaned up and eased into our robes for the night. I ordered a ridiculous amount of food from room service, as well as two bottles of expensive vintage wine.

When the food finally came, we attacked it! We were ravenous and tore through the myriad of delicious options shamelessly. We quickly moved on to dessert without missing a beat.

After dinner, we put on one of our favorite murder documentary shows and glazed over. It had been a long day, and we were exhausted.

I dreamt of dinosaurs that night. I always dream of dinosaurs when I'm feeling anxious. I don't know why, but I always do. Giant, lumbering lizards, dramatically larger than they would be naturally, stomped over the top of my head, threatening to crush me under their massive claws. I'm always looking up at them, threatening clouds above their heads, cracking with lightning. They never notice me, and it's not the threat of being eaten that grips me, rather being casually stepped on without them even knowing. I scurry around between their legs, trying to maneuver my way out of danger, but inevitably a giant, clawed foot always comes crashing down on my head!

This instance was no different; only when I awoke, startled and sweaty, my phone was vibrating. I picked it up and saw Natish's name flashing across the screen.

"Hello, Natish! How are things?" I was barely awake but could sense the urgency on the other line.

"Put me on speaker, Logan. Tess needs to hear this too." I obliged and shook Tess awake.

"What's the good news?" I asked jovially, knowing there probably wasn't any.

"Well, it depends on your perception of 'good news.'"

Tess, rubbing sleep from her eyes, became alert in an instant, "It's Bryce, isn't it?"

"It is," Natish admitted. "Looks to us like he's scoping both our houses on the regular with what looks to be some pretty rough-looking Russians."

"Oh God, I'm so sorry Natish." Tess lamented as she shrank into the sheets, holding back tears.

"No, it's okay! So far, we're on to them, but they aren't on to us being on to them - other than us breaking out their windows that one time, of course. They have switched to tinted sedans instead of SUVs, so they think we're none the wiser. Fucking amateurs. You guys leaving town, and having Mike and Cannon look after the house, has thrown them for a loop - but they are definitely planning something for sure," Natish's voice trailed off into grim territory on the last few words. "We've been in contact with the police, but they can't really do anything. They said they would be contacting the FBI, but who knows what that looks like."

"Jesus, the FBI!" I was stunned. "I'm starting to get fantastically worried here."

"Don't be - yet," Natish reassured. "Mike, Cannon, and our PI have been trailing them in rotation and discovered some *very* interesting things. Apparently, our boy Bryce has been skimming off the top and doing side deals behind the Russians' backs. While that's enough to get the Russians interested, the police and FEDs don't have enough to go after them yet. In any case, our PI is already talking to one of the Russian contacts, whom he is familiar with."

"Wow, that's a damn mouthful!" I was astounded they had compiled that much info in such a short amount of time. "All that in just 3 days, I'm impressed! You guys are safe, and there's no immediate danger, right!?"

"Yeah, we're good for now," Natish promised. "We sent Nanny and the kids to New York indefinitely - just in case, and we've been operating pretty fluidly since. We feel certain Bryce will be forced to run or learn how to breathe underwater once we deliver our proof package to the right Russians."

"Damn, this is like some kind of spy movie!" I could sense the tension in Tess's words, but she seemed somewhat relieved. "I can't help but feel like this is all my fault."

"Honey, this clown was at our house regardless; it's personal on many levels beyond you and Logan."

"Just be careful, you guys!" I pleaded in a worried tone. "We'll be back in two days, so let us know if there's anything you need. And please, again, just be careful."

"We got this, you guys! Y'all be careful too, and we'll see you when you get back. We should have a solid plan of action by then!"

"We are forever in your debt," I said, sounding like a cheap sales man.

The dinosaurs seemed closer than ever now.

Tess was noticeably fretting during the ride over to meet with John. She was taught like a tension wire, and I could feel the gears turning. "Try not to worry, Tess; Natish and the gang can handle themselves. I also have a private investigator I can call to help out their PI. He's really good - former navy intelligence. Very smart."

Tess snapped out of her daze, "What can we possibly do against the fucking Russian mafia!?"

"Well, that's the good news; we're not doing anything *against* the Russian mafia; we're helping them out. They will be grateful and will take care of our Bryce problem for us." I was trying to reassure her, but I could see the real danger presented by our situation.

"There is a lot that can go wrong with that plan, and it seems incredibly risky to me!" Tess was not convinced. "And you have your surgery next week! Oh God, this can't be good!" Real panic was starting to creep into her voice, and it hurt my heart.

"Don't worry about my surgery; I've had it twice before, and it's not that big of a deal. A few stitches, some gauze wrap for a week. It's not like I'm laid up for more than a couple of days."

"Still, the timing couldn't be worse, and we would do well not to underestimate Bryce. He may be a wannabe gangster, but he is absolutely dangerous."

"So am I," I said in my best action hero voice.

Tess looked at me solemnly but couldn't hold the intensity and burst out laughing. "No offense, but you're about as dangerous as a sunset."

I looked at her intensely, "I'm Batman..."

We both broke out into uncontrollable laughter. "You definitely know how to lighten the mood, Logan Lepozod."

"Well, that's my superpower!"

"It definitely is," Tess said while leaning over to kiss me on the cheek.

"Seriously, I won't let anything happen to you, me, or Natish's family. I'll call Paul, my PI, later and have him coordinate with Natish's PI. Paul is incredibly resourceful and brilliant. He'll know exactly what to do. In the meantime, I'm starting to get pretty nervous about meeting with John."

"Just keep repeating he's not a Russian gangster, he's not a Russian gangster...and you'll be fine."

"Good advice."

Tess was kind enough to drive the rest of the way to John's while I called Paul. He was excited to hear from me since it had been a few years. I apprised him of the situation and gave him Natish's contact info. He assured me he would help out in any way he could. I texted Natish once I hung up with Paul to get her up to speed. She texted back immediately that she would coordinate between Paul and her PI. Apparently, the PI had a fair amount of evidence to bring to the Russians once the time was right. Paul had some valuable contacts within the Russian mafia as well, so things were looking up.

Just as I was starting to feel better about that situation, we pulled into John's driveway. In a rush, the butterflies were back in force.

I had been hiding from this for so long that I was presently more eager to have it resolved than I was continuing to avoid it. Pull the trigger, I thought. My body seemed glued to the seat, but after a moment and a deep breath, I pulled myself up from my spot and exited the vehicle. It was like blasting off into space.

Tess made her way around the SUV and quickly took my hand, "You can do this! You both deserve some closure, and remember, you're Batman."

"I'm Batman," I repeated from far away. I suddenly snapped back to reality, grabbed hold of Tess's hand tightly, and we walked up to the front door of his charming, well-kept, little ranch-style home. I stood there for what seemed like an eternity and finally knocked.

John's front door swung open immediately, and there he was, a completely different person! I hardly recognized him. Painfully obvious was the lack of any smile or pleasant greeting. I anticipated this, and it was entirely understandable.

Gone was the polished, posh exterior he once had. It was replaced by an old, dusty plaid shirt and work pants. His hair was much longer, he had a very bushy beard, and his hands looked tired and rough, like old concrete. It was a little jarring, but I suspect I won that contest.

His eyes widened when he saw my face, and I could tell he was simultaneously sorrowful and pleased. I had given him as much of a head's up surrounding my condition as his communication had allowed, but he didn't give me a lot of latitude in the way of a warning.

"Well, well. Look who's here to unburden himself after all these years. Mr. Beautiful!" John was curt, solemn, and deeply burdened himself.

"I think we could both use some unburdening, John. May we come in."

"Oh, you and your incredibly attractive girlfriend, Tess? But of course!"

Tess, always a bright light, smiled authentically and held out her hand, "Hi John, it's nice to meet you!"

John responded without a handshake, "Charmed."

Tess, still smiling, withdrew her hand politely. He turned and walked into the house, leaving the door open. I imagined this was as close to an invitation as we were going to get. John's house was small but lovely. Very clean, practical, with a lot of niceties. It was largely in direct contrast to his dirty, weathered appearance.

"You'll have to forgive me; I just finished a job and wasn't able to clean up in time," John said sharply. "You want some coffee?"

"That would be great, thanks," I tried to say pleasantly.

The kitchen was directly adjacent to the living room, so John motioned for us to sit on his couch as he prepared the coffee. "So what, are you dying or something? Trying to make amends?"

I cleared my throat, "Um, no, I am not dying, but you are right; I am here to try and apologize."

"You were right, you know?" John said matter-of-factly.

"...About what," I asked softly.

"About my trying to hurt your career." John bowed his head ever so slightly. "I went to that auction with the sole intention of relentlessly trashing you for no other reason than it would have elevated me and my career. You just happened to outsmart - and out fuck me. The real catch is, I only have myself to blame."

"John, we were different people back then - " I started, but John cut me off.

"I felt like such a miserable, fucking piece of shit the whole time we were together."

John continued with vitriol, "I knew that you were aware of my intentions, but you were so precise in identifying my weaknesses; who I really was, and just so damn convincing of our love that I was riddled with guilt for setting out to hurt you." John stopped and took a deep breath as he poured the coffee. After a moment, he continued, "Honestly, when you publicly shamed and exposed me, I was relieved. Your fake love made me hate myself."

"It wasn't fake, John. I've hated myself ever since too. I understand what I put you through."

"Oh, you do, huh?" John slammed down our coffee as emphasis. "You have no fucking idea of what you put me through! My guilt during our relationship may have dissipated over time, but it was how you made me question myself later - who I was and where I fit into the world, that was truly devastating! I still can't trust anyone thanks to you! I am alone, with no friends, and terrified of any relationship because I can't let myself trust anyone ever again. My family disowned me after they learned of our... *relationship*, and my career was over the minute that interview aired. You single-handedly obliterated me with such panache and style, but only after I tried to destroy you in my clumsy, ignorant and naive way. So I guess my life now is recompense. You left me a furious, rotten, and forever soured man. Cream and sugar?"

Tess and I both nodded "yes" because we were too stunned to speak. John gracelessly dropped the sugar and cream dish in front of us. I found it entirely sad and ironic that John had placed himself in a prison that was very similar to my former prison.

"What I did left both of us in a perpetual state of self-loathing. I'm so sorry, John."

"Don't you dare condescend to feel sorry for me!"

His statement cut to the heart of me, but I let the wound bleed. "How can I not feel sorry for you!? I left you mired in the same swamp of insensibility I've trudged through all these years. I can relate! I can understand!"

"The Hell, you say! You don't get to feel sorry for me, Logan," ropes of throbbing veins stood out on John's neck. "Here you are with your fucked up face and your beautiful fucking girlfriend - both clearly, *deeply* in love, to rub the salt of that love right in my fucking eyes! And all this like you just strolled sweetly through life's unpleasantries - us, your condition, *EVERYTHING* - straight to your reward of love and continued wealth, waiting for you at the end. Fuck you, man!" John wasn't exactly crying; it was more like liquid fury excreting from every pore.

"I'm going to stop you right there, John," I spoke softly but confidently.

I measured my next words very carefully, "First of all, I am sorry. I'm sorry you felt like you had to drag me through the mud to elevate yourself, and I'm sorry I dragged your heart through Hell as retribution." My words cut my tongue as they came out.

"I'm sorry for all the lasting pain that you and I both felt - and feel - as a result of our past poisonous chemistry. I'm sorry I ever treated someone as wickedly as I did you; I will forever be ashamed of myself. I'm sorry we waited so long to confront one another; we deserve closure. I'm just...sorry." Tears began to flow down the rocky slope of my face, and I was trembling, but there was no stopping now. I knew this would be part of the price I had to pay.

"I did love you, John. Sincerely. I got scared is all. I wanted to call off my plot a hundred times because I had fallen so deeply in love with you, but I was weak and fused to my anger. Back then, it was all or nothing in my world. Ironically, that's why I...did what I did. I wanted to destroy something beautiful before it could destroy me by vanishing. I was...preempting destruction. I was a coward."

John fired back, "That's the most sincere thing you've ever said to me...ever, but it's too little too late! It's very easy to offer sage words from a lofty position when you're on the other side of the pain and in love again!"

"It's never too late, John," I promised, "and I am far from the other side of pain. However, I am not sorry I'm in love. I will never apologize for what I have because I fucking fought for it tooth and nail! I'm still fighting, goddammit! That's why I'm here! No matter what you've gone through or what you've done, it is possible to evolve - to be a better person and be loved by others again. Please don't reduce my journey down to a simple stroll through difficult times. It has been, and still is, an agonizing process of hardening myself, shedding my skin, and being vulnerable all over again." My vision swam; it was all so surreal that I struggled to wrap my head around it. Nevertheless, the dam had burst, and the valley was flooding.

"There is no playbook for this, John. There is no right or wrong way to do this; there is only stitching up the old festering wounds, amputating the diseased limbs, and trying to crawl toward something better. I am not asking for forgiveness here; I'm asking you to take the first, hard steps toward healing yourself. You are still special to me, John. That part has endured. That's the only part that matters to me now."

John thought long and hard for a moment, "Get the fuck out of my house."

I stood sharply, "Don't let what happened between us define who you are. I did for a very long time, and I suffered. I even blamed my deformity on you; I was so certain it was a form of...celestial retribution, punishment for my evil nature. I locked myself away for five long years and would still be locked away if not for Tess. She saved my life. I may have helped you over the ledge, but I can still help you back up." John scoffed as I pulled a business card out of my wallet and laid it on his coffee table. "Call me, John. I can help."

"Go. Just go." John managed, holding back a tsunami of tears. "Sorry, you wasted your time coming here."

"It was only a waste of time if you sit here for the rest of your life feeling sorry for yourself."

Tess grabbed my hand and quickly walked me out of there. The door slammed behind us. I took a deep breath, "Fuck."

"Just give him some time, Logan. He'll come around. I probably shouldn't have come with you." Tess squeezed my hand.

"I needed your support and strength to face him. I never would have done it on my own," I sighed. "My mouth hurts like Hell with all this talking to deaf ears."

"He was listening, Logan. I promise. Even if he never contacts you again, he heard what you had to say. Both of your prisons had no locks, just open doors waiting for you to have the courage to step through." Tess hugged me tightly. "He'll step through. He isn't your responsibility anymore; it's up to him now."

"I wish he had a Tess to hold his hand through the journey," I lamented.

"He does - you."

"Then I just let him down in a major way."

"You just keep being there for him; he'll find you when he's ready."

Chapter Eleven

Under the Knife

Logan

I spent the better half of the trip home on the phone with Paul, trying to coordinate everything for when we returned. Tess drove pretty much the whole way back, which was a godsend considering how much I hated driving.

Paul had been working with Natish's PI, Chuck, and they had a compelling plan put together. A week after my surgery, Furious, Paul, Chuck and I were to meet with Chuck's contact within the Russians at a place of our choosing, present him with the intelligence, and politely ask that they pull Bryce off our asses.

The Russian didn't seem to think that would be a problem, and in fact, he thought they would most likely be thankful for the intel. Paul and Chuck both felt we would never see Bryce again; in fact, no one would ever see Bryce again, and we were all just fine with that.

Paul said he had contacted the police one last time, but naturally, they were still no help. He even put in another call to the FBI, but they were very tight-lipped about their ongoing investigation and could care less if normal citizens were in danger. We were on our own.

In the meantime, the Russian contact, Kirill Sidorov, assured Chuck and Paul he would pull Bryce off surveillance of our houses and make sure he didn't act against us, but that we needed to back off as well. He was adamant about no more talking to the cops or FEDs; he didn't want this thing coming to a head before we could hand over our intel. That intelligence was the only thing that could save our skins with the Russians. It was a very delicate situation, and he wanted to make sure his business associates had everything in order.

Paul and the others were very concerned about doing the meeting so soon after my surgery, but I assured them all - ad nauseam - that I would be fine.

The only difference is I would have to go back to wearing my hood over the gauze bandages. I would be more supervillain than the supervillains. The irony was definitely not lost on me. I didn't care; I wanted, needed, to be there. Both Paul and Chuck reluctantly agreed. The four of us would hand over the information to Kirill and one of his associates while Natish and Tess hold up at Natish's house with Mike and Cannon. They weren't too keen on the idea, being strong independent women, but it just felt safer - right or wrong.

The very next day, I was off to the hospital for my surgery. Tess was there with me, comforting me with her bright and supportive soul. I was starting to believe in my worth again, and I had her to thank for it. This surgery felt like shedding my cocoon for a final time before emerging a changed man. It was all so metaphorical.

I had a lot going on, but I couldn't help thinking of John. I kept telling myself he just wasn't there yet, but that he would be some day. In any case, it felt like the wound was healing now, instead of hanging open, raw and festering. I'll take the scar over a septic lesion anyday, it reminded me that healing is possible.

Tess and I sat in the pre-op room hand-in-hand. She smiled so sweetly, basked in the warmth of orange light pouring in through the window from a spectacular sunset outside.

"I love sunsets," Tess whispered to no one in particular. "This is a good one too. Makes me feel like everything is going to be alright."

"Everything will be alright, Tess, "I reassured her. "You'll see. We'll have many more sunsets to enjoy together in the future."

"Isn't it *me* that's supposed to be comforting *you* before surgery?" Tess chuckled.

"You are, simply by being here. I love you, Tess."

Tess tilted her head to look me in the eyes, "I love you too, Logan." She then kissed me with lips that were warm from the sun, and it felt like a promise.

The physician's assistant suddenly walked in, "It's time, Logan."

I took a deep breath in, found my legs, and stood. "See you in a few hours, my love."

"Yes, you will."

The physician's assistant had me change into a gown, then led me to a stretcher and had me lay down. I wasn't too nervous, having had several surgeries before; rather, I felt impatient. I wanted to get this over with so we could get past the situation with Bryce, and we could all move the Hell on with our lives. I respected the journey, especially if it meant a life with Tess, but I was punch drunk from all the recent changes. I needed to catch my breath.

The surgeon came in and talked with me for a few minutes before they wheeled me into surgery. He marveled at how much I was speaking and how well. He assured me it would come much easier after the surgery, which would be a fucking welcome relief. My tongue had become really swollen and sore from all the talking after being silent for so long.

As the staff hooked me up to a myriad of monitors, my mind floated back to Tess, sweet Tess. Always Tess. She had saved my life.

The anesthesiologist tapped into my IV and asked me to count back from ten. As I counted, my mind was still on Tess. She saved my life...she saved my...life.

I had a dream. It was a wonderful dream. I dreamt Tess and I had a child. I dreamt of us at a BBQ with Natish and Furious, our kids playing. I dreamt of my paintings hanging in galleries again. Tess had her own successful restaurant, and Natish was working on getting her a cooking show! I felt such love, warmth, and peace. Then I was unceremoniously shaken awake by a nurse.

"Mr. Lepozod," she kept saying. "Mr. Lepozod, it's time for you to wake up now!"

My eyes popped open, "Welcome back," she said.

There was no way I could speak with all the sutures in my mouth and the gauze wrapped around my head like a python, so I nodded my head in response.

The nurse stepped back to allow Tess, Natish and Furious to lean in.

"Hey darlin', how ya feeling?" Tess said with honey in her voice.

I gave her a thumbs up before Furious grabbed my hand! With a wink, he said, "There he is! There's my bad motherfucker!"

"Honey, please stop quoting *Pulp Fiction*!" Natish begged. "Try to remember you're in a hospital."

"I know, I know," Furious said, laughing. "We're just glad you're okay, brother. We missed you two while you were gone."

I tried to speak, but it did not go well. Instead, I signed to Tess, who translated: "It's so wonderful to see you all! It means so much to me to have you here. The last two times I did this, only my," Tess struggled with the word for a moment...until - "Ah! *The accountant* came to see me." Tess frowned, "Well, you have a real family now, and we love you!"

"Damn right! Nanny is already asking about you and wondering when she can feed you back to fine," Natish said through a chuckle. "Nina hasn't stopped asking about you too. I had to promise her you would hunt Pokemon with her again real soon!"

At this, I enthusiastically shook my head 'Yes.' I signed to Tess again, and she spoke for me. "Are they still in New York?" Tess translated.

Natish hesitated a moment, "Yeah, until we can square this Bryce situation and get it handled." Natish became a little stormy, "I'm not gonna lie, this has me slightly rattled."

I tapped my chest as if to say, "me too."

Furious spoke confidently, "Relax, you guys! Chuck and Paul have it all sorted. They'll get Kirill to deal with Bryce, and he'll get what's coming to him. All we're doing is handing over some information. Easy peasy, lemon squeezy."

Tess and I looked at one another while smiling wearily with our eyes. Could it really be so simple?

"Always the poet, Furious." Natish joked, trying to bring levity back to the room.

I signed to Tess again, "Where are we meeting with them and when?"

Furious began to speak, but Natish jumped in over the top of him, "A week from tomorrow, you, Furious, Chuck, and Paul are going to meet Kirill and his associate at the Hilton Carlton Hotel bar at three PM sharp."

Furious rolled his eyes, "What she said."

Natish continued seamlessly. "As you know, Tess and I will be waiting at my house with Mike and Cannon. We have a meeting with Chuck and Paul at your house in four days to go over everything and make sure you boys don't screw anything up. I hope it's okay we told everyone your house; we figured you'd still be resting up."

I tried to smile, but it hurt my face, so I nodded.

Furious interjected, "Don't worry about that now! Just get some rest, and we'll come to see how you're doing tomorrow."

"Please, try to take care of yourself and don't overdo it," Natish asked sincerely. "None of us is thrilled with any of this, but you need to take care of yourself."

I signed to Tess, "I'll be fine, been down this road several times. Just a few stitches, but I'll be right as rain in a week."

Tess leaned down and gave me a huge hug and a kiss on the head, "You better be!" I hugged her back with all my might. Truth was, I was in a lot of pain, and it would be a miracle if I was ready in a week.

Tess

Logan slept like a baby because of all the pain meds, but I laid awake all night, tossing and turning with everything that was on my mind. Not only was I worried about Logan, but I was consumed with fear and guilt over the Bryce situation, which was what we were all calling it now.

Natish kept telling me she was thankful I let them know a bastard like him was in their circle, but I wondered if he would have just eaten, left, and vacated their lives forever had I not been there for him to recognize. Then there was that little voice in the back of my head, amplified by Natish, that reminded me he was a sex trafficker of women and was in desperate need of...justice.

The Russians would most certainly eliminate him for skimming and side-hustling, so it was basically like we were pulling the trigger. I considered how I felt about that for a quick second - a very quick second. I wondered how many other women had fallen prey to him. How many underage women? How many little girls? He was so charming and diabolical; surely, his list of victims was a long one. Then it became less about feeling guilty for handing him over to the executioner and more like I wanted to be the one to drop the ax myself.

As peace surrounding that resolution blanketed me, my mind conjured something else to worry about. Logan. Not only his surgery but his uncompromising stance on attending the meeting.

The thought of something going wrong with him and Furious there made me sick to my stomach. There were ten million different ways the whole thing could go sideways, and only one way it could go right.

Chapter Twelve

Paintings and Horror Movies While You Wait

Logan

My face and mouth were killing me, but in a way that I knew it would be over in a couple of days. As I said before, I'd been down this road several times, and it was always the same: brutal pain for about three days, then a slow subsiding, like the tide rolling out. I was still concerned about being ready for the meeting, but I felt confident I could make it work with a little help from our friend Oxy.

In the meantime, there was nothing for Tess and me to do but wait. We couldn't even have sex because of the pain meds and the fact that my face was wrapped like the invisible man. So, that left one thing: painting and horror movies.

Tess cued up a horror movie, and I painted. I was very close to finishing the BBQ painting, which I figured I'd give to Natish and Furious. They kept going on and on about how much they loved it, and I wanted to gift them a painting for being such good friends anyway. I asked Tess how she felt about it because I knew she loved it too, but she thought it was a very nice gesture - as long as I painted a portrait of her and me to hang here in the house. I was given explicit instructions not to sell it or give it away!

It would be only the second painting I ever did of my condition. *Disgusting Faced* was my first and last to date. I found it entirely surreal that it was hanging in Natish's office. Every time I was over there, I had to go and sneak a look at it. Natish always busted my chops at how I would creep up on it like it was going to bite me.

God, I was such a different person back then; sad, confused, angry, scared...I had painted myself as a dark, wicked, macabre figure, slightly obscured by mysteriously freakish and terrifying shadows. The portion of my face in the light was even more terrifying, with twisted knots of flesh and lumps of porous lipomas. Jesus, I didn't ever want to be that person ever again! That said, I really did like the painting, even if it represented such a grim time. More importantly, I loved it because Natish and Furious loved it.

Natish and I had talked very seriously a few weeks prior about her representing me, and I finally pulled the trigger! I was on the fence at first, but Tess assured me it would be therapeutic and proffer me a sense of purpose again. She was not wrong! After signing with Natish, I was already hot to start a new series of 14 paintings, as well as a few sculptures!

Natish was a powerhouse in her industry! She had already done a ton of research, had an incredible strategy for my return, and was planning several showings in esteemed galleries, too much anticipation.

Even in my prime, Matilda had not been able to get me into a few of the galleries Natish had set up. I couldn't believe she was able to get me in! Especially since I hadn't been on the hot list for a long time. She explained to me that they were so eager to host my return show that she didn't even have to push that hard. According to Natish, there was a great deal of interest in the art world surrounding a new series of mine! I couldn't believe it!

Natish was very humble about everything she had done for me, but I wasn't about to let her downplay it. All the more reason to gift her with a painting!

Tess paused *Day of the Dead* in order to use the bathroom and check out the painting so far. I was mere moments away from finishing it!

Tess gasped as she put her hand over her mouth, "It's absolutely beautiful, Logan! It makes me want to cry! It's like your mind took a Polaroid of that day. All the subtle gestures and poses are so characteristic of everyone. You captured everyone's likeness so well! The colors are so rich and draw you in. You're so intuitive and aware of every tiny detail! I mean, *LOOK* at the stonework there and the patterns in the tablecloths; it's exactly as I remember it! Natish and Furious are going to absolutely love this!"

My mouth was still a disaster, so I signed to her, "I'm so pleased you like it and appreciate all the details! You are an incredibly astute critic! I'm really flattered by you!"

Tess wrapped her arms around my shoulders and drew very close, "I guess we can be pals then. And I only understood about a third of what you just signed. I've been slackin' thanks to your yackin." She kissed me lightly on the gauze covering my lips, which I finally had thanks to the surgery.

I signed, "I love you," and grinned as best I could.

She kissed me again, "I love you too. So, what are you going to paint next? You've got a series to complete now, thanks to your big comeback!"

I didn't sign; I simply pointed to her. She immediately turned crimson red, and her eyelashes fluttered furiously, "You don't have to paint little ole me to make me love you!"

I shook my head and signed, "I know, but I'll paint you because you..." and now I tried speaking, "sex...me...up."

Tess playfully slapped my arm and kissed me again. "You dog! Will you paint yourself with me? In the painting, I mean, not actually painting yourself with my body. I want you to paint an image of yourself in the painting of me. You get it."

I couldn't help but laugh. I held her head in my hands and stared deeply into her eyes. I spoke again, "Nothing would make me happier." I winced a bit at the pain.

"Stop trying to talk so much! This is my grand opportunity to speak unfettered by your responses. Hahahahahahaha."

I held up my left finger as if to say, "hold on," and with my right hand, I dipped my brush into a dollop of red paint and did my signature in the left lower corner of the painting, LL.

Tess clapped her hands and squealed like a teenager! "So exciting! Are you going to take a break after this one?"

I spoke, "Hell no!" Then I saw the look in her eyes and decided to sign the rest, "I took a five-year break; I'm awake now and ready to keep the momentum going! Next up, you and me!"

Tess leaned in for another kiss, “Guess we kind of changed each other’s lives, didn’t we?”

I spoke, “We sure did.”

Chapter Thirteen

Big Trouble in Little Jersey

Logan

Four days after my surgery, I felt a lot better. I was still in the bandages and was still having quite a bit of pain, but I could speak comfortably for a few minutes. Past that was a challenge. Tess and I were even able to enjoy a little light lovemaking the night before, which was very nice! I swear, I could spend eternity between the sheets with her!

Natish called us after breakfast to confirm we were all getting together that evening to rehearse our big day. On speakerphone, she said they would bring a huge dinner so we could eat our fears. I wasn't complaining. Tess heavily rolled her eyes, but I knew she would crush a three-meat plate. Haha! "Crush," she was definitely rubbing off on me. I assured Natish we would be ready around 5 pm for everyone, reminded her to bring extra hot wings, and quickly hung up the phone before Tess could argue.

"You know, Logan. Clandestine rendezvous with Russian mobsters isn't necessarily an excuse to binge eat."

I laughed internally, "clandestine rendezvous," I was rubbing off on her as well.

"Yes, well, I'll skip the Snickers!" I would, too; I had come too damn far with my training to fall off the Snickers wagon. Still, I absolutely planned to have some wings and ribs!

"I guess we better do some light training to offset the extra cheat day," Tess quipped.

I groaned ostentatiously but figured it couldn't hurt since we were apparently international spies now. We had some good routines and moves for a couple of crackers on the Cape, that's for sure! Apparently, Natish was rubbing off on me as well.

"My head kind of hurts..." I said sheepishly, vying for a pass.

"We'll be sure not to do anything that will involve your head, kay? But I'd like to run a few of those Russian fighting tactics and routines again," she said, being totally serious.

"Oh man, do we gotta?" She responded by hitting me in the stomach with just enough juice to unbalance me. "Okay, okay, it's on!" I said. I came at her skillfully, but she quickly had the better of me. She was kind enough to let me get a few moves off, then promptly humiliated me again. Tess was actually a very talented fighter. Bryce must have been particularly surprised by her resistance and level of skill. Fucking punk like that will always wilt when stood up to.

Tess

After an hour or so of training with Logan, we cleaned up and got ready to have everyone over for dinner. Part of me wished so deeply that the dinner was just that, a dinner and not some strategy meeting leading up to a dangerous encounter with criminals.

God, I hated that I had even dated that fucking tool, Bryce! I can't believe I slept with him either! Ugh, so gross. At least I used protection...and it was over fast. In any case, we just had to get past this one thing, this one huge, monumental obstacle in our path, in order to move on. Nothing major, just the Russian fucking Mafia! Oh God, I was begging for a panic attack.

Logan came out of the bedroom with his hood on, which caught me off guard a little since I had gotten so used to him without it. He read the concern in my eyes and gathered me up into a big hug. He felt like home. After a moment, he put his hands on my shoulders and began vigorously massaging them. He was always such a comfort, and I moaned like an old, rusty gate, "Awwwwwwww, dear God..."

"Looked like you were on the verge of starting to worry," Logan said sarcastically, his words coming much more easily now. I could tell he was relieved by it, saying earlier that he enjoyed talking now that he had people worth talking to.

"You're very perceptive! Aren't you worried about all this?" I couldn't imagine he was as calm as he led on.

"I'm terrified!" Logan loudly admitted, then winced from the pain. Dialing it back a notch, he elaborated, "I have faith that everything will go smoothly. We're simply handing over some information in a very public place and getting the hell out of there. We'll be fine."

His words pacified me some, but I was still very much on edge. "Bryce is very shrewd, and we would do well to remember that."

"Good advice," a familiar voice said from the failing light in the back hallway.

Logan and I spun around to see Bryce standing there with a gun! He had four mean mugged men with him that looked like they were etched in stone. Fuck. Me.

Logan and I both reigned in our absolute shock and horror admirably, but our hearts were racing a million miles a minute! "Well, well," I said in my calmest voice, "It's the real Slim Shady."

Logan stepped in front of me, "What the fuck are you doing in my house?"

"Nice hood, Meatball! Glad someone clued you in! Am I too early for your little get together?" Bryce asked smugly. "I apologize for that, but I wanted to make sure we got here first, you know, so we could greet everyone as they arrive. I'm pretty hungry too; I've been craving hot wings and ribs like you can't believe," he finished saying with a pompous little laugh.

Logan stiffened, "I'm so glad you're in the know. I guess you're already aware that we've been working with the cops and the FBI as well?" Logan lied as best he could.

"Oh yeah, we know all about that. Although to say you're 'working with them' is a bit of a stretch. Our friends in local law enforcement have assured us that there is no ongoing investigation and that the FBI is about as close to nailing us as they were three years ago. Sorry, Mr. Meatball, but you're all on your own."

Logan, never losing his poise, played our ace, "Well, my friend is friends with your friends and has instructions to deliver our intelligence straight to them should anything happen to *any* of us."

"Ohhhhh, wrong again. I assume you are referring to your friend Chuck and his friend, Kirill?" Bryce's smile widened.

Logan somehow managed to maintain his unwavering resolve, but my heart sank into my bowels, and fear gripped my spine with icy fingers. I had no idea if I was giving it all away with my expression or not.

"I'm impressed! I detect no fear from either one of you!" Bryce shook his head. "However, if I were in your shoes right now, I'd be pretty *fucking* terrified. One thing you don't have to worry about, though, is that we wouldn't show up to dinner without bringing dessert! Vigo..."

My stomach fluttered as one of Bryce's guys stepped forward with a large cake box, wrapped with a bow, in his hands. The box looked incredibly small and absurd in Vigo's massive mitts. Bryce, relishing his moment, did the honors in opening it...

There, inside, was a bloody man's head with milky eyes turned up towards the ceiling and an impossibly swollen tongue in his mouth. "Allow me to introduce Kirill Sidorov!" Bryce announced, showcasing the grotesque horror with both hands like he was presenting a prize.

I instantly turned my head and puked, but Logan held firm. Bryce laughed, "I guess I found your limit, huh, Tess? You're one tough bitch, I'll give you that, but ain't no bitch tougher than a severed head! I'm surprised Mr. Meatball here still has his balls! Not for long, though; I plan to hang them from my rearview."

"I guess that's one way to get some balls, fucking pussy," Logan wisecracked ubelievably.

Vigo snorted, and a little laugh slipped out. "Sorry."

Bryce stared daggers at Vigo for a moment, then turned his attention back to Logan, "Hey asshole, *I'm* the one with the gun!"

"Did it come with an extra four inches for your small cock?" Logan asked dryly.

Without warning, three of Bryce's goons burst out laughing. "SHUT THE FUCK UP!" Bryce screamed! They quieted, but the impression was they had about as much respect for Bryce as we did.

Logan continued to try and bluff, "If you think Chuck and...*Kirill*, we're our only aces; you're wrong, buddy."

"Oh, c'mon now. I think we all know those two guys were your only aces. Going all-in on pocket aces before the flop is always so... *risky*. Sure, you have a lot of opportunities to scrape the pot in the end, but there are also a lot of opportunities for shit to go sideways - kind of like it's going right now, for the two of you and all your pals."

"You have no idea what -" Logan began, but Bryce cut him off.

"Shhhhh," Bryce put his finger up to his lips. "Let's just have a glass of that single-malt scotch I see over there and wait for your buddies to join us."

"Sounds like a party," Logan said gruffly.

I was so proud of Logan for holding it all together, but I had never been so scared in my entire life. All the horrible scenarios I had run in my head up to this point were nothing compared to the reality that was materializing before my eyes. I had just seen a severed head, for fuck sake! I felt like I was gonna pass out. I didn't know what to do with myself!

Logan

Bryce had drawn all the curtains, sat Tess on one side of the living room, and me on the other. Tess and I were able to subtly sign to one another without them noticing, but we didn't want to risk them catching on. I told her not to worry, that we would figure it out. She responded that she trusted me, but she would be looking for an opening to escape, so be ready. I told her to watch for my signal.

Bryce was kicked back in my favorite chair, sipping my favorite whiskey, and just so damn happy with himself. His goon squad, all armed, loomed ominously over us. There was nothing we could do to escape at that point or warn the others.

Bryce had our phones and passwords, so he was responding to Natish and Furious, telling them all was set, and we couldn't wait to see them!

Bryce finished a large gulp of my expensive whiskey and took note of the BBQ painting. "Heeeeey, I remember that day! What a lot of fun, right! You know what, though, it's missing something...Me!" Bryce picked up a red paint tube, squirted out a hefty glob, and dipped a brush into it. "I'm not as good a painter as you, Logan, but I have some skills! Here, let me show you!"

I narrowed my eyes and stared right through him, but before he could ruin the painting, our doorbell rang. Here we go.

Bryce dropped the brush back onto the palate, pulled out his gun and motioned for his goons to hide in the hallway bedroom. "In case you're getting any thoughts of heroics..." Bryce manhandled Tess up off the sofa, got behind her and stuffed his gun into her ribs. "Answer the door and invite everyone in. We'll be hanging back, but I'll be watching. Any bullshit, and this bitch'll be breathing through a hole in her chest. Understood?"

"Understood," I said through clenched teeth.

Bryce soundlessly mouthed the word "Yay" and slinked back into the hallway bedroom. I got up, moved over to the door and opened it. Everyone was there, standing on my porch with goofy smiles on their faces. Natish and Furious had arms full of food, Chuck had a couple of 12-packs, and Paul was holding a bottle of wine and a briefcase full of intelligence. Damn, he did bring it with him. Fuck!

Furious hollered, "There he is," and everyone poured into the house, laughing and talking amongst themselves. Natish was yelling at Furious to be careful with the food; Furious promised he wouldn't drop it, and Chuck asked where to put the beer.

Paul was last inside; he grabbed up my hand and shook it vigorously, "Hey man, great to see you again! How is..." He trailed off when he saw my face and quickly went to pull out his gun. Unfortunately, one of Bryce's goons emerged from behind me with his gun pointed at my head. He shook his head "no" and collected Paul's gun. The goon slammed the door, and everyone snapped their heads around to look at us. In an instant, everyone's smiling faces dissolved into grim frowns. Natish and Furious dropped the bags of food to the ground and focused on the guns pointed in their direction.

Que Bryce! He walked out like a porn star with Tess's arm firmly grasped in one hand and a .45 in the other. "Hey! Everyone's here! Excellent!" He looked over to Chuck, "Wanna hand your smokewagon on over to Vigo there?" Vigo came up behind Chuck like a storm cloud, clapped one massive meat hook onto his shoulder, and extended the other, palm open past his face. Chuck took a deep breath in, slowly pulled out his revolver from a shoulder holster inside his jacket, and handed it over to Vigo. Bryce practically yelled, "Yay, now we can all be friends!" He shoved Tess into the living room, where we were all standing, as the rest of Bryce's goon squad circled around us.

Bryce walked over to Paul and gently put his hand on the briefcase, "is this what I think it is?"

Paul, "It is. However, all the copies are somewhere safe with an associate of mine who has explicit instructions to deliver them to your bosses should anything happen to us."

Bryce clapped a hand over his mouth and feigned shock! "Heavens to Murgatroyd, whatever shall I do!?" He tip-toed flamboyantly over to a table that had Kirill's head in a cake box on it and produced another cake box. Uh oh. "You mean...*THIS ASSOCIATE*!?" Bryce flipped open the cake box to reveal another severed head.

Everyone collectively gasped in utter horror! Natish could have passed for a statue, and Furious looked wild-eyed and ready to pounce. I hoped I could figure something out before he went ballistic.

"Jeeeeeesus Christ," Paul managed. "There's a thumb drive -"

"Oh, this one!?" Bryce pointed to a thumb drive stuck in the dead guy's mouth. "Yeah, your boy gave it up after I pulled out his toenails. Sorry dude, but if you didn't think I would be monitoring all of your phones, emails, fucking grocery lists - ugh! It's obvious we aren't operating from a position of mutual respect here."

Paul thankfully took the reins, having had some experience in this arena, "Okay, you got us. What now?"

"Well, I'm awfully glad you asked me that, Paul - yes, I know your name. It just so happens that I have a penchant for the dramatic, as you may have guessed by now, and a keen desire to send a message. Would you like to know what my message is?"

"Lemme guess, don't fuck with you." Paul was trying to keep him talking, so I was trying to think fast.

"Bingo!" Bryce proclaimed.

Chuck suddenly spoke up, "What about Kirill? I assume he's how you found out about all this."

Bryce answered gleefully, "His head is in the other cake box, *Chuck*." He emphasized Chuck's name jovially and smiled a wicked smile.

"Gosh. Pretty risky cutting off the head of Vladislav Barinov's nephew," Chuck said in a condescending tone. "He was considered a valuable, sanctioned liaison between law enforcement and the Russian Mafia - which is how I know him. It's also why the Russians liked to keep the fact that he was a liaison, AND Barinov's nephew, kind of quiet."

Bryce suddenly looked a little dewy on his brow. "Bullshit."

"Okay, whatever you say. A quick call could clear that right up for ya, though, huh, Vigo?" Chuck said patronizingly. Vigo and the other three goons now tensed up a bit as well. It was subtle, but they were eyeballing each other. They obviously didn't know Kirill was so high level.

Chuck continued in stride, "Annnnnywho, last time I checked, a sanctioned law enforcement liaison was pretty hard to come by. You know, if you guys don't have Barinov's number, I'd be happy to give him a call; he's on my speed dial." Chuck had found the weakness he needed in the group and was trying to exploit it to drive a wedge and buy us some time. "Hey, Vigo, this fuckin' twerp just put you right in Barinov's crosshairs. Y'all too," Chuck said, pointing at the other goons. "Probably ought to do a little checking around on folks before you go chopping their heads off."

Bryce suddenly blasted a hole in Chuck's stomach! "Oh noooo! Owwwieeeeee! Gut shots smart like a sonofagun! Probably ought to shut the fuck up, huh?"

Natish cried out, "No!" But quickly turned back into a statue.

Chuck crumpled to the floor, holding his belly, "You cocksucker! I'm too tough a piece of meat for your tender teeth! You better get mommy to spoon feed you some -"

Bryce shot Chuck in the head. Natish turned and buried her face in Furious's chest as he looked straight at me with big, round eyes. His eyes said he was going to act soon. I motioned my head ever so slightly to indicate I was with him.

Tess was also transfixed on me with the same look in Furious's eyes. I signed to her to get ready to run.

Paul quickly motioned subtly for us to wait, "What's your plan here, Bryce? Kill all five of us here in suburbanville, get rid of the bodies, and then try to hide the fact that you killed a guy much higher on the food chain than yourselves? Then just hope and pray this never gets out, and all goes away? Vigo, you and your pals are going to be sucking cement real soon thanks to this douche canoe, unless you can get out in front of it, and *quickly*."

"SHUT THE FUCK UP!!!" Bryce screamed at Paul, shaking his gun wildly! "These guys have all been in on everything with me from the start! They were already in the shit the minute they helped me skim. We've all got so much shit on each other; we have to be family. They ain't gonna help you."

Paul decided to shut his mouth and get ready to act. He looked at me and gave me the eye; it was time. I nodded that I understood, then gave Furious the eye, and finally gave Tess the sign!

Tess

Logan gave me the sign, and my heart stopped. I didn't like the odds. Five to five, their favor. I mean, they were trained killers for, fuck sake! I hoped more than anything that our Monday morning YouTube kung-fu would hold up. I had my doubts, though. In any case, we had little option; these motherfuckers were definitely going to kill us one way or the other, so we may as well go down fighting.

I watched Logan with eyes that hadn't blinked in 20 minutes. My blood was pumping nitro, and I was ready to pounce!

Paul moved first! Vigo was slightly behind him, and to the right, so Paul spun around, smacked Vigo's gun and sent it flying! Clearly, Vigo wasn't expecting us to attack. Vigo instantly reacted by trying to slug Paul in the face, but he was big and slow! Remarkably, Paul was able to dodge it and was only grazed. Paul then unleashed a flurry of impressive moves that took Vigo by surprise, but the sheer size of the Russian allowed him to absorb most of the impacts. Paul was nimble, though, and was able to avoid most of Vigo's lumbering moves. They locked up and struggled! Paul saw Vigo's gun on the floor and went for it! I only hoped Paul could grab it in time.

Logan was next to act and to the left of Paul and Vigo. He stomped the side of Vigo's right knee with his left foot, and there was a loud pop! Vigo crumpled, and Paul dove for the gun!

Bryce leveled his gun at Paul, but Logan was on him in an instant! He tackled Bryce to the floor and was on top of him like a linebacker. Bryce was completely caught off guard and dropped his .45 in the melee! Unfortunately, it slid across the room before I could grab it.

The other three goons were slow to react, likely thinking we would never fight back. I tripped one goon headed for

Logan, who went down hard, face-first; then I lept into the air like a crazed tiger, onto the next goon! I sunk my thumbs into each of his eyes with every bit of force I could muster as I rode him down to the ground! He shrieked like a schoolgirl, and I knew I had him!

I pulled my right thumb free from his gouged eye, balled my hand into a tight fist, and dropped it like a wrecking ball directly onto his Adam's apple, crushing his windpipe like a cardboard tube! He gasped, dropped his gun, and clapped his hands over his throat, struggling for air!

Furious suddenly soared through the air as a professional wrestler might and dropped his elbow squarely onto the cervical spine of the goon I had just tripped! He was out like a light!

Goon number five opened fire wildly! We all dove out of the way and took cover, but it was only a matter of seconds before one of us got shot!

Then the strangest thing happened, the large panoramic window in the living room exploded and showered glass everywhere! Goon number five flew out of his shoes and came to rest in a heap on the floor. I wasn't about to wonder why!

Without hesitation, I bolted like a gazelle to the coat closet, stepping right on eye-gouge goon in the process, flung the closet door open, and grabbed Logan's shotgun! I racked a shell into the chamber and looked for - anything!

Logan had Bryce in an arm bar, and Furious was sitting on top of his unconscious goon like it was story time in first grade. Paul had found Vigo's gun and trained his sights on the

Russian bear, his eyes saying everything: move, and you're dead.

With all the baddies taken care of, everyone looked wide-eyed at the shattered glass window!

"Don't shoot!" a strangely familiar voice shouted out! "It's John! Don't shoot; I'm going to come in through the front door, okay!?"

Logan responded in a bewildered tone, "John!? Holy shit! Yeah, please...uh, come on in!"

John slooooowly opened the front door and peeked inside. "I'm coming in, don't fuckin' shoot me!"

"It's okay," I said, "you can come inside. We won't shoot!"

John crept inside like a plaid covered secret agent, with a Desert Eagle .50 in his hands, pointed at the floor. "What the Jesus H. hillbilly cornbread Christ is going on around here!?"

Logan stuttered, "It's ah...It's a long story, John. Super glad to see you again, though!"

"Yeah, well, that's a story I'm going to need to hear. I just called the cops, and they're on the way." We could already hear the sirens closing in. "Please tell me the guy I just shot is bad."

"He was bad, John. He was very bad," Logan reassured him.

"And who in the fuck are these guys!?" John demanded, pointing at the Russians.

"Bad guys, John." Laughing a bit now, "Bad guys."

"Well, they fucking better be, considering I just used my hand-cannon to put a hole the size of Candle Stick Park in that guy! Fuck sake! I guess it's a good thing I felt bad about how we left things. How *I* left things."

Logan caught his breath, "I'd say so. You just saved our lives. Thank you."

Natish snapped out of it and quickly ran over to Chuck, "Ohmygod, Chuck!? Oh, you can't be dead!" Tears were streaming down her cheeks as she kneeled down to check his condition. Everyone sadly turned their heads to watch Natish try and shake Chuck awake. "Chuck! Chuck! C'mon, man, wake up!"

Furious climbed off the goon, who was still completely unconscious and slowly comforted Natish. "It's okay, honey. We'll take care of him."

Natish suddenly shot up with fury in her eyes and zeroed in on Bryce! "You fucking piece of shit! I WILL FUCKING *KIIIIILLLLLLL YOOOOOUUUUUUU*!!!!!" Furious grabbed her in a bear hug and held her tight as she fought wildly to get free.

Bryce stopped struggling at this point and stared at the rug. Logan climbed off of him, and I pointed the shotgun right at his head. "Please, please give me a reason," I said in my best action heroine voice. Bryce snorted and lay there quietly.

Natish calmed down, wiped her eyes and stolidly addressed Bryce, "You just fucked up big time, pal. I will not rest until you fry for this!"

Logan, now standing, addressed everyone, "Hey guys, just hang tight; I'll go talk to the cops."

"You better take that hood off so they don't think *you're* the criminal mastermind," I said, half-joking but totally serious.

"Fair point," Logan said and took off the hood, his face still wrapped in bandages. "Any better?" He asked.

"Here," I handed Logan the shotgun, "*I'll* go deal with the cops."

"Probably a good idea," Logan sheepishly agreed.

Logan kept the shotgun trained on everyone's best buddy Bryce while I went out on the porch, hands up, to talk with the hundred cops who had just coalesced on Logan's lawn!

The police captain jumped out of his car with his service gun drawn and ordered me down on the ground! I obliged but yelled at him to call an ambulance.

Logan

Tess was on the porch trying to calm the police captain down- as well as 99 cops - and explain what was happening while I tried to get myself together and keep Bryce from misbehaving.

Vigo started cursing under his breath and getting restless, so Paul tapped him on the head with his shoe, "Hey, asshole, shut your cry hole." Suddenly, Chuck choked and drew in a loud raspy breath! We all reacted with total shock, but it was Natish and Furious who rushed to his side!

Natish, "Just relax, Chuck! Don't move! I knew you were too mean to die!"

Chuck was dazed and in a lot of pain, but it appeared the bullet had either ricocheted off his head or only grazed him! This guy needed to play the lottery.

Furious took off his shirt and pressed it against Chuck's head, who was trying to talk and starting to squirm.

"Lay still, brother! Don't try to talk! Just hang in there; help is on the way!" Furious looked worried but hopeful.

In an instant, every cop in the tri-state area poured into my house! They were all yelling at everyone to be quiet, get down, and put our hands behind our heads!

We all did as we were told, but Bryce started hollering out that he needed help and was the victim here! The audacity of that frosted flake was astounding. The cops ordered him to shut up, then fitted everyone with zip-ties.

It took a while to get everything sorted out, but we all gave our statements, and the Ruskies, along with Bryce, were roughly escorted out and into an armored transport unit. I wasn't sorry to see them go. Natish, Furious, Tess, Paul, and myself were un-zip tied and allowed to relax a bit. A hazmat crew had to come in and remove the heads, fucking ghastly.

I couldn't believe the activity in my house! Only three months ago, it was the quietest, darkest house in the state, but now - it was a damn three-ring-circus! Cops everywhere, the FBI finally showed up (better late than never, I suppose), and medics were working diligently on Chuck to get him stable so they could move him to the hospital. The goon John had shot was dead as a doornail, and the one Furious dropped his elbow on was still out cold.

Natish and Furious were allowed to go home. They resisted at first, but Tess and I promised to touch base with them first thing the following day. Paul was instrumental in helping law enforcement wrap their heads around everything that had happened. It didn't hurt Paul and Chuck were friends with some of the local cops.

He did inform the FBI that the local cops were compromised, so the FEDs took over the investigation and called in Internal Affairs. That was going to get messy.

Paul left with Chuck in the ambulance, and there were a few straggling investigators puttering around. One finally came up to Tess and me while we were sitting dumbfounded on the couch and informed us that we would have to leave and stay at a hotel so they could examine the house...which was now an active crime scene. They also told us not to leave town. Yeah, no shit.

John finished giving his statement and trudged over to us, grumpy and exhausted. "Fucking drive 10 hours to your goddamn house, kicking myself for being such a bastard, only to arrive and hear two clear gunshots. I'm like, oh shit. Fortunately, I have - had a big ass gun in my glove box! The biggest one I could buy! I have my conceal and carry, anyway, I creep up to the front window, and through the curtain I see this big ass Russian with a gun start shooting wildly at you guys, and I'm like, oh shit, oh shit! So I fucking blasted him. Shit, I killed a man tonight."

"You saved our lives," Tess said with absolute gratitude. "You came here to talk it out and ended up saving our lives. You are a good man, John. I guess we can be pals."

We all burst out laughing. "Christ Logan, I bet this one keeps your ass in line," John said affectionately.

"And then some," I admitted. "I just hope Chuck is okay. I'm sick about it."

John thought on it for a second, "Gutshot, he should be fine. Lucky son of a bitch, fucking bullet richocheted off his hard head, at least that's what the Feds told me."

"Unbelievable. Actually, believable from what I know about him. He's hard as a coffin nail. Wanna stay at the Hilton with us? Separate rooms, of course. My treat, the least I can do...You know, for saving our lives and everything."

"Haha, Logan, this girl is definitely rubbing off on you. You were such a tight-ass prissy little bitch before. Now, look at you, 'coffin nail,' who are you?" John couldn't stop himself from laughing. This got us all going again. What that must have looked like, the three of us in a bloody crime scene, laughing our asses off. Who are *we*?

"You're not wrong, John." I held out my hand, and he shook it. "Let's go to sleep real soon."

"I heard that," Tess said, getting in between John and me, hugging us roughly! "Shame all that damn BBQ went to waste."

We all looked down at it and sighed, then I noticed; my painting was still standing perfectly unmolested on the easel, except for one little thing; a bullet hole right next to my signature. I laughed. "Hey, look at that," I said, pointing. "Now, I'll have to sign every painting that way. Neighbors are gonna love that!"

"And they were just getting to know you. Cest la vie." Tess smiled and gave me a huge hug and a kiss. "How is your face?"

"It's perfect," I said. "Perfect."

Epilogue

Tess

A little over a year later...

I was jolted awake by thunder, Logan lying next to me.

Snow was hitting the window in sheets so thick you couldn't see through it. I always found it beautiful and unusual when it thundered with lightning during a snowstorm. That's Jersey for you!

A quick flash unexpectedly filled the room, followed by an ear-splitting crack of thunder! Logan shot up like a dart in bed, "Whaassssat!?"

I put my hand softly on his shoulder, "It's just thunder, baby. No worries. You can go back to sleep. It's late."

Logan looked out the window. "It's thundering and snowing!?" He asked like a six-year-old.

"Uh, yeah. I know, pretty cool, right!"

"I looooooove thunder snow," Logan said in a childish voice. "C'mon!"

"Wait, what!?"

"Come on! Let's go out and look at it!"

"What, now!? Are you serious?" I started giggling. "It's 3 in the morning!"

"I know, come on!" Logan was out of bed and putting on his robe and slippers. "Let's go, my love!"

"Okay, gimmie a second, and we'll go look at the thunder snow!" I put on my robe and slippers, and we crept down through the house like thieves, so we wouldn't wake John C. Jr. Yep, the "C" stood for Chuck. "You don't think the thunder will wake Chuck, do you, baby?"

"It will definitely wake him up," Logan whispered and chuckled almost inaudibly. "So, let's go look before it does!"

"Okay, okay, hold your horses. I never knew you were such a child at heart. Friggin' thunder snow." I actually love thunder snow too, but I couldn't let him know that.

"Shhhhhhh! You know you love thunder snow," Logan whispered. "Don't even try to hide it."

"Okay, I do love thunder snow. I'm not a monster after all."

We got to the back door and threw it open like a couple of kids. The snow was coming down in huge, wet flakes by the billions, and the sky, purple, angry and dark, crackled and popped with intermittent lightning and thunder. The purplish light, highlighted with lightning flashes, impossibly lit up the night when reflected off the deep snow.

The snow was also so dense that there was almost no sound at all, except for the sound of the big fat flakes hitting the ground. The only other sound was so enchanting and surreal; it was like being in an alien world. All the tree limbs in the surrounding woods were creaking, groaning and snapping under the weight of the thick and heavy snow. It was the most beautiful thing I had ever seen and heard. The percussion of snow, and wailing of the trees, were almost like a siren's song. A bit sad, but beautiful. There's no way I can describe the image and sounds and do it all justice.

I looked at Logan and smiled such a peaceful smile. My whole life was about this moment right here. Being here with him, with our son, with all our friends and growing families, it felt like love.

Logan was back in the art world full force and was doing even better than before! Natish had declared war on Logan's former agent, Matilda, and was crushing her best talent with Logan's new series entitled: *The Ones We Love*. He and his paintings were the talk of the town again, only this time, he was being praised and admired for his bravery and philanthropy instead of his exclusivity and shrewdness. He and John even did another interview for Adrian Seerlie's new Vodcast, which, again, shattered all his top viewership numbers. John still lived in South Carolina but had a new hunky boyfriend that we got to meet a few weeks ago during a visit down south.

Nanny and I had joined forces to open a restaurant specializing in New Orleans cuisine and soul food, and it was doing really well! Thanks to Natish and Logan, the buzz had reached as far as the west coast! Natish was in talks with Gordon Ramsey to do a holiday special, and there were big plans to have additional locations opened in New York and LA! Logan was always creeping around the kitchen, trying to sneak food, but I had him on a healthy diet and a tough regimen of exercise. Saturdays were his cheat days.

Logan's health was great; his condition had slowed substantially and was more manageable thanks to his surgery and subsequent treatment. I loved him and our family so much that it filled me to bursting. I was so thankful.

"You know this thundersnow is the second most beautiful thing I've ever seen in my life," Logan said genuinely. "I love you, Tess."

"I love you too, baby. I love you too."

The End

About Author

I live in North Carolina with my beautiful wife, who is the one that got me started in the romance world, and my step-daughter. I work as a CT tech during the day but my true love is art. I am an artist and writer at heart. I enjoy bringing my characters to life and challenging my writing skills by changing genres. I love living in the mountains and hiking but have lived all over the country and enjoy writing about all of these varied locations.

If you would like to follow me and find out what is next you can find me at linktr.ee/jwereboi

Made in the USA
Middletown, DE
24 May 2022

66155890R00099